Jenny came out of the bathroom as Danni walked into her bedroom. Jenny stood still, not knowing what to do. Then she saw what she had been yearning to see. There was no way that Danni could mask or deny what Jenny now saw on Danni's face, in her eyes.

Danni could feel a throbbing in her throat. She couldn't tear her eyes away from Jenny's body. She wanted to feel that exquisite flesh. She wanted her, all of her. Slowly, she walked over to Jenny. Slowly, she moved her hands down her back, feeling the sensuous line, and rested them on her hips.

Her mouth was dry; her voice was husky. "You haven't dried yourself." Her fingers traced a bead of water down Jenny's throat . . .

Horizon
of the Heart

Horizon of the Heart

Shelley Smith

The Naiad Press Inc.
1986

Printed in the United States of America
First Edition

Cover design by The Women's Graphic Center
Typesetting by Sandi Stancil
Editor: Katherine V. Forrest

Library of Congress Cataloging in Publication Data

Smith, Shelley.
    Horizon of the heart.

    I. Title.
PS3569.M537976H6   1986   813'.54   85-25892
ISBN 0-930044-75-4

For each other

Shelley Smith is the pseudonym of two writers living in the Boston area. Partners since meeting in 1981, HORIZON OF THE HEART is their first collaborative work.

Horizon
of the Heart

I

Danni Marlowe walked across the living room to the sliding glass door. A golden glow spread across the sky as clouds on the horizon held the promise of a beautiful sunset. She took a cigarette from the pack in her hand, tapped it against her thumb and reached for a lighter at the corner of the table.

"What do you say, Duvall?" she said to the dog dozing on the rug nearby. "Walk? Want to go for a walk?"

As she opened the slider, Danni didn't bother to turn to see if Duvall was behind her; she knew he was. Beyond the lawn stretching from the back of her house to the sea wall some twenty yards away rolled the sea, turning on the late afternoon tide, pulling in its wake sand, shells, small pebbles. At the water's edge, Danni dropped her cigarette, watched it float along the edge of shore, then disappear.

"Find a stick, boy," she called to the dog.

Obediently, he ran along the shore line of the beach and soon returned with a piece of driftwood in his mouth.

"Good boy. Now drop it. Drop it, Duvall. Du-*vall*!"

She stepped toward him, reaching for the stick, and the tug-of-war began. Every muscle in his one hundred and fifty pound body tightened as he grasped the wood between his teeth.

"Think you can keep it, huh? I'll show you who's boss." She tugged, he pulled. Back and forth their bodies shifted, Danni's feet sinking into the wet gritty sand to keep a foothold, the strength in Duvall's huge body pulling her forward.

Finally, bored with their game, he dropped the stick. "Good boy," she said, reaching for it with one hand, brushing her thick shoulder-length blonde hair back with the other. She threw the stick as far as she could and began to walk in the direction the Great Dane ran.

Reaching into the pocket of her slacks for another cigarette, she noticed two figures on the sea wall a short distance away: a little girl sitting cross-legged, tossing a ball back and forth in her hands, a woman beside her, a tennis visor shielding her eyes. The curly-haired child drew Danni like the glow of the sun; had she ever seen such a head of burnished gold? Suddenly, the child jumped down from the wall and ran toward Duvall.

"Sara! Sara, come back," the woman called.

Danni waved. "It's all right. He loves kids."

At the shore line Sara and the dog met eye to eye. Duvall dropped the stick he'd retrieved and sniffed the red rubber ball she offered.

The woman hopped down from the sea wall, walking quickly to the small girl. A sudden gust of wind lifted her cap and blew it across the sand. As rich auburn tresses tumbled in the wind, Danni saw immediately how the child had come by her beautiful hair. The cap rolled her way and Danni stopped to pick it up.

"You can't be so trusting, Sara," the woman said, taking the child by the hand, her voice soft and gentle.

The girl reached out tentatively to pat Duvall. The dog's wet nose ran across the palm of her small hand.

"Look Mommy, he likes me."

"Yes, he does like you," the woman said, "but all the same, I don't want you touching strange dogs."

"But he *really* likes me!"

The serious expression on the child's face broke into a brilliant smile. My God, Danni thought, what a beauty.

Cap in hand she walked toward the two of them, unable to take her eyes off the child. What a find for the Nature's Secret ad, she thought. Something that will *sell* shampoo, they said, something special. Well, if she's not, I don't know what is. And if she can act a little for the TV cameras, we'll have a real prize.

"Your hat, madam," Danni said.

"Thank you for catching it," the woman replied.

"You're welcome." Danni smiled and extended her hand. "I'm Danni Marlowe. And the friendly beast is Duvall."

"Well, hello to you both. I'm Jenny Winthrop. That's Sara over there with Duvall. I have the feeling they could become best friends."

Her smile was dazzling, just like the child's, but broad and trusting as well.

"They seem to be getting on just fine," Danni said.

"Aren't they, though?"

Jenny brushed her hair back from her face. Flecked with gold and amber, her eyes were as green as a black cat's, the lashes thick and long. Bedroom eyes, Danni thought, no doubt about it. Her complexion was like a Dresden doll's — clear, delicate, flawless; her mouth was full and sensuous.

Just then Duvall, the red ball in his mouth, turned and

began running toward the house.

"Duvall," Danni called, her attention diverted. "Get back here. Now! I'm not fooling!"

But Duvall was out of sight.

"So much for obedience school," Danni said. "How about walking back to the house with me so I can retrieve Sara's ball?"

"Oh, it's all right. She has others —" Jenny felt a dryness in her throat as she tried to finish the sentence. The woman standing before her was tall, blonde, cool; her eyes were chips of cold blue ice. Her stance was haughty, arrogant, yet there was a compelling sensuousness about her. When she smiled, as she did now, Jenny saw the expression of a shy child on her face.

There was a moment of awkward silence. "Poor Sara. She's been wanting a dog for the longest time." Jenny felt her words run senselessly one into the other. "Now she won't be happy till she has one just like yours. Which will be never, of course. My goodness, how much does he eat?"

Jenny was conscious of the beating of her heart. Knowing how easily she blushed, she wished she could turn away as she felt the color rising to her face. Instead she blurted, "Maybe someday she'll be able to have a cat, but a dog — it would never work out — they have to be walked all the time, don't they?"

"Well," Danni said laughing, "not *all* the time. What do you say, Sara," she said to the child standing at her mother's side, "let's go after that bright red ball of yours. I don't want Duvall thinking he can get away with that kind of trick," she continued, turning to Jenny. "And since the sun's well past the yardarm, I'd say it's time for a drink. How about it? I just live up the way." She gestured toward her home, a large white Victorian set back from the sea.

"We're staying over there," Jenny said, "in the yellow house."

"Grace Ash's place?"

"Yes. We'll be there for some time, I expect."

"How do you and your husband like it?"

"There's no husband," she said decisively. "I'm divorced. But we like it just fine, don't we Sara?" she asked, her arm around the small girl. "A friend of mine knows Mrs. Ash. When she went out to Arizona, it seemed perfect for us."

"Has it been?" Danni asked.

"As perfect as could be," she answered, pausing before she finished the sentence, "for the two of us."

"Strange we haven't run into each other on this stretch of beach before," Danni said, "but then I guess I'm not around much."

"Mommy, can we go see the dog?" Sara asked.

As red and golden hues streaked the late afternoon sky, the two women looked at each other.

"Sure," Jenny said. "Why not?"

* * * * *

Danni opened the slider. The three of them stepped into her living room — a designer's dream but a housekeeper's nightmare. There was clutter everywhere: clothes, papers, glasses, overflowing ashtrays.

Danni walked to the sofa, picked up last Sunday's *Times* and invited Jenny and Sara to sit. "Don't mind the debris," she said. "One of these days I'll get around to cleaning this place up."

Duvall appeared at the door. Danni took the ball and tapped him on the nose a few times. He walked into the room, then regally stretched out on a maroon Persian carpet.

"Here you go, Sara," she said, tossing the ball to the child. "What do you say? How about a Coke?"

"Do you have any juice?" Jenny asked.

"Sure do. And how about you? Scotch? Bourbon? Gin? I make a pretty fair martini."

"Would you happen to have any wine?" Jenny asked.

"Of course. White or red?"

"White. Please."

"One juice, one white wine and one very dry martini coming up," Danni said, leaving the room.

Beyond the living room, Jenny saw a formal dining room, a large foyer and stairs leading to the second floor of the spacious house. What a lovely home, in spite of the clutter, Jenny thought. Oak bookcases, their shelves full, lined one wall of the room. A Victorian lamp of garnet leaded glass drew her attention to a graceful mahogany table. Above a white marble fireplace hung a large abstract painting, vivid colors bursting across the canvas. As the glow from the sun bathed the room in rich golden tones, Jenny leaned back against the sofa and thought, How comfortable it must be living here.

Danni returned, placing a tray in the center of the coffee table, brushing magazines to the floor to make room.

"In the words of my favorite actress," she said, "*what* a dump!"

Both women laughed. "Not at all," Jenny said, "this is a wonderful room."

"Aren't you kind," Danni said as she sat in a rose velvet wing chair, crossed her legs, and looked about the room in objective appraisal. Beneath the clutter there were lovely antiques, family pieces all, given to her by her mother. She wondered what her ancestors would say if they could see them now.

The air in the room was stale. Too many snuffed butts, Danni thought. Got to stop smoking. Water rings formed patterns on the end table beside her. Not totally uninteresting if you were into water rings. She reached over and drew a line through the dust and chain of rings. It's time to slow down on the booze, too.

As if she'd been reading her mind, Sara looked up and said, "Why is your house so messy, Danni? My mommy would be mad at me if my room looked like this."

Danni laughed. "Mine would be too, sweetie. I usually try to clean up when I know she's coming."

"That's enough, Sara," Jenny said. "Drink your juice."

"Staying at Grace Ash's must be pleasant for you," Danni said, taking her mind and the conversation off the subject of her poorly kept house. "I knew she'd gone out to visit her daughter after her husband's death last August; I didn't realize she was still with her."

Jenny said, "Oh, yes, she's very happy out there and we're certainly happy being here."

"Good," Danni said, "though Baysville does seem a bit off the beaten track for someone like you."

"Like me?" Jenny asked, smiling. "How so?"

"There's a big city called Boston only twenty miles from here that offers a hell of a lot more excitement than this town."

"Assuming I want excitement," Jenny said.

"Who doesn't? At least a little. You're not from around here, are you?"

"No," Jenny said, "we're from New York —"

"New York?" Danni exclaimed. "That makes it even *more* of a mystery —"

"There's no mystery to it at all. After the divorce I thought about what I wanted to do with my life and where I wanted to spend it. Raising a child in New York City is not the easiest thing in the world . . . I have friends in New England . . . and a good friend in Boston."

"The person who put you in touch with Grace Ash?"

"Yes. So with what I'd managed to save and child support and —"

"Don't feel you have to explain," Danni said. "I'm not prying."

"I know you're not. That's why I'm telling you," Jenny said, surprised at how easily she talked with someone she had known less than an hour. She raised her glass, finished her wine. "Anyway, I thought I'd better get to work carving out a future for Sara and me."

"Housesitting?"

Jenny laughed. "I'm a student these days, finishing course work for an art degree I began long before I married."

"Commercial art?" Danni asked.

"No," Jenny said, "I'm in Art Ed at B.U. I come from a family of teachers. If I ever finish the degree and am lucky enough to find a job, I hope to be as fine a teacher as my mother was. Her field was science, but I've fancied myself an artist since I was a child. It was a way of working out my fantasies, I guess. And housesitting was one way to stay ahead of the astronomical rents in Boston. Baysville's been real good for Sara. She loves kindergarten and she's all set to start first grade in the fall. Aren't you, honey?"

Jenny glanced at her watch. "My goodness Sara, we've got to run. I told Beth I'd pick Stephen up by six-thirty. Say goodbye to Duvall for now and don't forget your ball." She looked at Danni. "I'm baby-sitting for a friend this evening; I have to pick up her little boy. It's a good thing too, or I'd have sat here the rest of the evening boring you with the story of my life."

"What makes you think you were boring me?"

Jenny smiled. "Guess the wine went to my head."

"It's easy for that to happen," Danni said, smiling back. "I'm glad we met, Jenny."

"I am too. I hope we see each other again."

"We will," Danni said, "I'm sure."

She opened the slider for them, holding Duvall by his

chain so he wouldn't follow, and watched them walk down the lawn. She took another look at the living room. What's the matter with me, she thought. Why can't I be in a room more than ten minutes before it becomes a shambles? But isn't that what housekeepers are for? If I don't find a new one soon I won't be able to invite *anyone* in here. Not that I haven't tried. It's Duvall, partly, but. . . . She remembered mornings when, heedless of any audience, she'd paraded from her bedroom without bothering to put on a robe, a young man in tow who wanted coffee. Other mornings when she stayed in bed long into the day nursing hangovers that she told herself she'd never suffer through again.

How could she expect any housekeeper to understand? And why bother? It was always so easy to get another. Housekeeper or man, she thought, though at the moment she was interested only in the former.

She'd call Mother tomorrow. There might be someone she could send over from Hope House. Problem was, they never stayed very long . . .

Hope House, a shelter for unwed mothers, had been founded by Ethel Marlowe four years ago. During that time Mrs. Marlowe had provided several temporary housekeepers for Danni. So far, none had been so tactless as to discuss her lifestyle with her mother. Or had she been kidding herself about that? Her mother never criticized her, though, and if she knew what Danni's life was all about, she kept it to herself. Nothing quite matches New England reserve, Danni thought wryly.

Her eyes focused on the tennis cap lying on the sofa. In the disheveled room, it seemed to be a point of order. Now there was a woman who seemed to have her life in hand — like her mother, whose life was also in control. Hope House was only one of several projects that received Ethel Marlowe's energy and support.

What's wrong with *me,* she accused herself. I'm thirty-eight years old and I live like a spoiled college co-ed. Except for the agency.

She was proud that in less than five years her advertising agency had become one of the most successful in Boston. There, she thought, sipping her drink, I'm Danielle Marlowe, founder and president of Marlowe Advertising. Why, then, doesn't it give me more pleasure? Why do I drink as if liquor holds the answer when it doesn't? She set her empty glass on the table. And sex? I know better than anyone that sex with strangers holds the promise of nothing but strangeness.

She did not allow these thoughts very often. When she did, depression followed. She did not want that to happen today.

Aimlessly she moved her right foot over a Persian carpet bought on a trip to the Middle East last winter. She thought, I've probably traveled more in the last ten years than all of my ancestors combined. All those miles. For what? The perfect fuck? Crude thought, but let's admit it, it's my only serious hobby, the only thing I really care about. Besides work.

She walked to the sofa and picked up the tennis visor. The campaign, she thought, holding the cap in her hand; I didn't even mention the Nature's Secret ad. I'll return this tomorrow and tell Jenny all about it then. I don't have any afternoon appointments; Garth won't be here till five. There's no rush. There's no chance she'll say no to what I'm prepared to offer her.

* * * * *

Danni saw Sara sitting on the swing on Grace Ash's front porch, a large coloring book on her lap, a box of crayons beside her.

"Mommy guess who's here," Sara called. "The lady with the dog." She jumped down from the swing, opened the screen door and ran down the hall, Danni following.

Jenny sat at the kitchen table shaking change from a large ceramic piggy bank.

"Hi," Jenny said breathlessly, in surprise. "Come on in. I'm just encouraging Miss Piggy to go on a diet."

Danni smiled. "She need to lose weight?"

"I give her a workout about once a month whether she needs it or not. Today, *I* need it."

"Short on cash?" Danni asked.

"Just a bit."

"Well, pass the hat."

Standing, Jenny took the visor from Danni. "How nice of you to bring it over. We were going to drop by but I didn't think you'd be home in the middle of the afternoon."

"I took the afternoon off," Danni said. "Mind if I sit for a minute?"

"Of course not. Would you like a cup of tea? I just brewed a pot from herbs Sara and I picked while we were out walking last week." Jenny felt nervous, excited. She hadn't expected to see Danni so soon. "I have coffee left from this morning — but you don't like cold coffee, I'm sure —" Jenny felt her tongue tripping over her words. When was the last time she offered someone cold coffee? "I could heat it," she said smiling. "Or better yet, make a fresh pot. It won't take but a minute."

"I'll have the coffee cold," Danni said. "I live on coffee that's been fermenting in paper cups for at least twenty-four hours. It breaks down the caffeine. Much better for you than herbal tea. Especially any herbs you'd pick around here. Haven't you noticed all the dogs?" Danni thought of her own brute.

"The herbs have been washed. And dried in the sun. I'm sure they're perfectly safe."

"Not as safe as cold coffee," Danni said.

"Okay. One cold coffee coming up. Sara, it's time for *Sesame Street*. Do you want to take a snack up with you?"

"No, Mommy, I want to watch my program," she said, scampering from the room.

Jenny was grateful for the chance to turn away from Danni. She'd felt riveted to the spot, held by her gaze. As she reached for a cup and saucer, she saw Danni's image reflected in the kitchen window glass. She felt a wave of giddy excitement at the vision. Determined to maintain her composure, she turned back to Danni. "Anything in your coffee?" she asked evenly.

"No thanks. I drink it black as the night." Danni smiled as she took the cup. Then the smile disappeared as quickly as it had come and Jenny looked into deep blue eyes that were unfathomable. Jenny filled her own cup from the pot of steaming tea and sat down.

"Jokes aside," Jenny said, "I may have to pass the hat before long." She blew on her cup of tea. "I had a call from Mrs. Ash this morning. She's decided to stay on in Arizona with her daughter. Her son already has a buyer for the house. She was very nice about it, but within six weeks Sara and I have to move on."

"Where will you go?" Danni asked softly.

"I don't know. I haven't had enough time to think about it, really."

"Good news usually follows bad," Danni said encouragingly.

"What do you mean?"

"Ever hear of Marlowe Advertising?"

"Yes, I have," Jenny replied. She recalled a newspaper article just last week that included a photograph of the striking president of the agency. "Is it your family's business?" she asked.

"No it isn't. Marlowe Advertising is my baby. Mine alone."

Jenny felt foolish. "Well, of course. I read an interview you gave the *Globe*. Your picture —"

"Those photos didn't resemble me in the least. Obviously." Both women laughed. "I mention it because I've been searching for a little girl for the Nature's Secret shampoo ad. It's one of our major accounts, we'll eventually handle all of their health and beauty products. That'll be big bucks, more than Miss Piggy could ever hold. From the little I've seen of Sara, I don't think I could find a better model for the campaign. Kids her age usually love to work; they're naturals."

Looking at Jenny, Danni had what she thought was a sudden flash of genius. Even to her professional eyes, this woman was perfection. Full-breasted, slim and graceful, she reminded Danni of a young dancer. Probably in her midthirties, she was beautiful, whatever her age. This time I've really hit the jackpot, Danni exulted. I'll use them *both* in the commercial. Why not? This had to be written in the stars — the timing couldn't be better.

"Actually, you and Sara would make quite a team. I'm sure you've had your share of compliments. Am I right?"

Jenny set her cup on the table. She could feel her body tense. The phrasing was all too familiar.

"It's just occurred to me, Jenny, we could design a campaign similar to the Breck mother-daughter shampoo ads of a few years back. With TV advertising, we'd have to devise some unusual dramatic scenes — various settings in the northeast, work in the different seasons. Summer wind. Autumn touch. Frost bite." She grinned. "No — scratch the last one."

Danni was enjoying the moment. She felt that she was reeling in a couple of very special fish. This had to be an exciting opportunity for the two of them. Besides, Jenny needed the money.

"I'd like you to come in for a screen test, say next Monday or Tuesday, but as far as I'm concerned, it'll be a formality. I'd sign you and Sara to a contract right now if I had the forms with me."

Danni was accustomed to seeing expressions of excitement, pleasure or even gratitude on her models' faces. Jenny just drank her tea. Probably in shock, Danni thought.

Jenny looked at Danni knowing too well the games advertising executives played to get clients, models, whatever else they wanted. She knew exactly the look Danni expected to see on her face.

"I appreciate the offer," Jenny said firmly, not wanting the game to go on any longer. "I've appeared in a Breck ad before." She waited for the expression on Danni's face to change, but it didn't. "I was with the Powers Agency for five years," she continued. "I decided a few years back that it wasn't the life for me."

"Why not? Didn't like living in the fast lane?"

"You could say that, I suppose." As Jenny thought back on those years, she felt anger rising within her. She stood and leaned against the kitchen counter. "There were just too many things to deal with. My life's simpler now. And it's my own."

"What was so complicated about modeling?" Danni asked, wondering why she wasn't trying to think of a way to pressure Jenny into taking this job.

"Complicated? The pace. The competition. The pressure. Drugs to stay thin, the sleeping around —"

"But the cash — didn't that help you forget the complications?"

"Oh, sure. When I was a kid. But I'm far from that now. And I spent the money I made — ever know a model who didn't? I stopped working when I was pregnant and when I went back a year later, I was old. Old at the age of twenty-nine," she said raising her eyebrows. "Old to the camera's eye."

She spilled what was left of her tea into the sink. "I could have continued to work, but the compromises — there was never any end to them. I don't want those values," she said angrily. "And now?" Jenny gestured skyward and smiled, her anger vanishing, "This time I'll finish that degree. No modeling — ever again. And none for Sara either." Jenny thought of what she'd just said. Not wanting to offend Danni, she added, "You were kind to think of us."

"I wasn't being kind," Danni said, surprised by all she had heard, "I was certain you two were the perfect answer for a very tough client. Talk about being over-confident," Danni added, laughing at herself. "That's what comes from working in a man's world."

Jenny acknowledged Danni's comment with a smile, but she didn't want to carry the discussion any further. "If you hear of any house-sitting jobs nearby, I'd appreciate it if you'd let me know." She sat scross from Danni and thought about what she was giving up by not taking the job, not in terms of salary — she'd already settled that issue and knew that somehow she'd manage — but by not giving herself a better chance to know Danni.

"As a matter of fact," Danni said, "I do know of a job. Not exactly house-sitting, but it's in the same ball park and pays better. Right here in the neighborhood, and you could start any time."

"You run a house-sitters' agency, too?" Jenny asked, a touch of a New York accent still in her voice.

"To tell the truth, my dear, not exactly," she said, mimicking the accent. "What it comes down to is I need a housekeeper. I *do* need a Nature's Secret model, but I need a housekeeper even more. My home's comfortable, I pay a better than average salary, and best of all I'm not around all that much. Your spare time will be your own — whatever you need for your studies."

Jenny smiled, thinking that she wouldn't mind Danni

being around at all.

"I put in very late hours, come home half in the bag, usually just fall into bed — and not always alone. But don't worry — with Sara there I'll be discreet. Besides, my bedroom's at the far end of the house. You should know that other housekeepers never stayed with me very long. If it's not me, it's the dog. But the way he's taken to Sara, that shouldn't be a problem."

Relieved, Jenny thought that Danni couldn't have been more on target: good news had indeed followed bad. "There won't be a problem," she said. "There won't be any problems at all."

"That's the spirit. And by the way," Danni said offhandedly, "Don't change your mind if you hear any local gossip about me. Let's give it a try first, okay?"

"Sounds fair to me," Jenny said, wondering what she meant by local gossip, thinking that there were a few stories about herself that Danni might find difficult to hear. But then, she and Danni hardly traveled in the same social circles.

They walked to the front door. Apparently hearing their voices in the hall, Sara ran down the stairs. Impulsively, Danni scooped her up in her arms and Sara hooked her scrawny legs around Danni's waist.

"Can I come see Duvall sometime?" she asked.

"Anytime you like. How's that?"

Sara hugged her. Danni felt a clean, wonderful surge through her body. The child smelled like hot toast. God, she thought, I could become addicted to this kid.

II

Garth Reynolds was his usual punctual self, arriving precisely at five. Danni was her usual self as well; she walked through the house half-naked, absently fastening her mauve lace bra as she looked for a spot to deposit her last cigarette before brushing her teeth. She dropped it into a vase of dead, brittle flowers.

"Know anything about smoke signals, Garth? Now's our chance to send a few." She sat down on the couch next to Duvall, trying with both feet to push him down to the far end. He wouldn't budge.

"My Boy Scout days are too far into the past to remember much of anything," he said, dropping his tall frame into the only chair in the room that wasn't covered with clutter. "If you're not careful, I'll have to go in search of your fire extinguisher."

"What fire extinguisher?"

His grey eyes reflected concern. "You don't have one?"

"Not unless it came with the house and I sure don't recall ever having seen one. How's this?" she asked, letting a slow trickle of wine flow from her goblet. "Don't want to waste too much, it's vintage Bordeaux. How do you like it, my sweet?"

"Not bad," he said, taking a sip.

"It should be better than that for the price I paid."

"Give it a chance to breathe."

"Sure," Danni said, picking up the vase. The mass of dried leaves and brown petals was smoldering. "I'll set this in the kitchen sink, that's safe enough."

Garth leaned back in the chair and stretched. He'd worked out at the club most of the afternoon. Though he was sore and weary, he knew it was a form of relaxation his body needed. As he sat there, he felt his muscles relax. A long swim or a fast game of racquetball allowed his mind to slow down, to put the administrative problems of the hospital in perspective. He felt loose tonight; it was a good feeling.

He'd changed at the club, leaving his suit in the car. He felt comfortable in his navy polo shirt and tan trousers. He ran his hand across his face. Not much of a beard, he thought. Guess I didn't need a shave after all.

In lots of ways, Garth was feeling his forties approach. This year he'd stopped smoking, got down to the weight he was in med school, and cut back on his drinking. He figured he looked a few years younger than thirty-eight, which wasn't bad for all the effort, though he knew his thick, dark hair was a natural asset. Told more than once that he was handsome, he'd never thought of himself as so. His chin just missed being protruding. "Strong," Danni had described it. Whatever — he didn't put much emphasis on his looks. As long as he could continue to count on his body to perform all that it had to do, he was satisfied.

He reached for his glass, stretched out his legs and smiled as the woman he called the love of his life walked back into the room.

"The wine's quite good," he said.

She laughed. "Must be it's had time to breathe." Again she tried shoving the sleeping dog to the far end of the sofa. "Damn dog," she said. "I bought him for protection. All he's done is destroy the house, take over my bed and lay claim to every other comfortable spot in the place."

"Get rid of him," Garth said, knowing it was the last thing Danni would do.

"How? Who would want him? Think we could find him a nice home somewhere out in the country?"

"We could try. If that's what you want."

She picked up her glass of wine. "We'll see."

As Garth glanced around the room, Danni could read his thoughts: the place was a mess. "Now don't be so judgmental, darling," she said.

"I didn't say a word."

"You forget, Garth, that a picture's worth a thousand words. The expression on your face right now would —"

"I thought I was a better poker player than that."

"Not with me you aren't. I can read you like a book. Good news, though. Yesterday I met the mother-daughter team that's been house-sitting for Grace Ash." She told Garth about Jenny and Sara Winthrop. "She's really got her work cut out for her here, wouldn't you say? When you see what a hopeless housekeeper I am, Garth, aren't you glad we never married?"

The two of them laughed.

When both were just a few months shy of twenty-five, they had made a formal announcement of their engagement. Two weeks before the wedding, they attended a dinner party given in their honor by Garth's parents. At first Garth didn't think much of the fact that Danni seemed to be among the missing; she'd been at the dinner table, but excused herself and didn't return for coffee and dessert. He remembered thinking that since they'd had drinks before arriving, she'd probably fallen asleep someplace, and that he wished she'd develop better control of herself at public functions — he'd seen too many doctor's wives with a fondness for liquor. Danni was nervous about the wedding, under too much pressure — at least that was the explanation she offered after he'd found her in the pantry in a compromising position with one of the waiters.

If his mother hadn't been just behind him, he would have gone through with the marriage. To him she was like a small child where sex was concerned, a small child whose body had become that of a beautiful woman. For Danni sex was part recreation, part exercise, part self-indulgence; fidelity was a word in the dictionary. All of this he knew long before their engagement, and although he could have killed the waiter she was with, he held no grudge against her. But there was no way that he could marry a woman his mother had then and there loudly proclaimed a whore. The waiter had backed off as Danni smoothed her skirt. Then she'd said in a cool, self-contained voice, "A picture's worth a thousand words, as they say."

Eventually, Danni's phrase had become part of their own private language and Garth was grateful for the relationship they'd been able to salvage. Even though they would never be husband and wife in the usual sense, he felt married to her. He knew he was her anchor in times of trouble; he kept her from drifting too far out to sea. She was all he ever wanted in a friend and he knew that no matter what happened in the future, he would never lose her. Too much had passed between them; too much was holding them together, not least of all the sexual relationship they still shared. No woman satisfied him in bed the way she did, and even though he might not be the most exciting lover she'd known, he had a staying power she found more than attractive. He had stopped thinking about the many men in her life and had the good sense not to tell her about the women who moved in and out of the circle of intimacy that was his own private life. No matter who he met, there was always room for Danni. Even during his two-year marriage he and Danni had remained close. In spite of her confidence, success, and drive, he knew there was still that little child in her who needed to be held.

"Garth," she said, interrupting his thoughts, "what do you say we have a quiet evening? Let's go down to The Mooring, get a table on the deck, have oysters and wine — You're not on call tonight, are you?"

"Nope. I'm all yours."

"Good. I'm in the mood to have you be all mine," she said.

"For tonight," he answered.

"For tonight," she replied. "We don't want to spoil a good thing after all these years, do we?"

He shook his head and she wondered: Why not? He was the most decent human being she knew, the only man she was always comfortable with. There wasn't even a question of whether she loved him or not; she knew she did. She saw him often, they spoke on the phone almost daily. She attended various social functions attached to his profession, and they were easy traveling companions, their annual jaunts to the Caribbean brightening the month of January for them both. She wasn't looking for anyone to take his place and now that she thought of it, her relationship with him was the only one she maintained.

"What do you think about getting dressed?" he asked, pouring more wine. "An early dinner is your idea. We'll have plenty of time to decide whether it'll be your place or mine."

"If you've got sheets on your bed, it's yours. Honestly, Garth, I've got to change. I'm like a fucking nomad on the desert of life. Or a shipwrecked sailor lost at sea. Or a —"

"Beautiful woman in the mood for oysters."

"Listen, I'm in the mood for more than oysters," she said leaving the room.

He thought about the softness he'd find beneath her satin bikini underwear before the night was over, and he waited patiently as Danni talked to him from her dressing room. Once again she mentioned her latest find in house-keepers. There were at least two problems she'd have to deal with, he estimated. First, the child. Her life-style didn't lend itself to school age children, no matter how captivating. The second and more intriguing question was the notion of this former-model-turned-housekeeper. Danni said she was gorgeous; that wasn't a word she used lightly. How long would she be content keeping house for Danni? And how long would she want to seek refuge in a town as small as Baysville? It's got to be a temporary arrangement for her, he concluded. He looked up as Danni walked into the room in beige slacks, a wine colored shirt, heeled sandals.

"Sure you want a quiet evening?" he asked admiringly.

They walked toward the door arm in arm. Danni said, "To you, my sweet, oysters may be quiet. To me, they're pure, unadulterated passion."

III

The Monday before Memorial Day weekend, Jenny and Sara moved into the wing off the second floor sunporch. Danni had calculated that she'd have all the privacy and space she needed on the first floor. The bay window in her bedroom opened to the east and there was a slider leading out to the patio and small garden where she spent much of her time during the warm months. Since the driveway was beyond the patio, the slider afforded a private entrance to her bedroom; after-hours friends she brought home could enter and leave that way. She didn't mention any of this to Jenny, assured that her own life wouldn't be disturbed by these two relative strangers, as attractive as they might be.

The morning Jenny and Sara arrived, Danni was running late for a meeting. "Hate to dash like this," she said, "Why don't you relax, unpack and just get settled today?"

"Do you know what time you'll be home?" Jenny asked.

Danni was taken aback by the question; she hadn't been asked that in years. Previous housekeepers had stayed as much out of her way as possible; it was doubtful any of them cared when she'd come back.

"I'm not sure," she said. "But I'll be home."

"Well, that's reassuring," Jenny said, smiling broadly.

It was obvious that Danni had tried to straighten up, but the place was a shambles. Jenny could live with it, though. She'd known people like this before: attractive, successful, well-organized professionally, yet their homes, expensive showplaces that they might be, became their personal dumping grounds — as if the coil of their daily lives unwound once they walked in the door and tensions disappeared totally. You couldn't hold it against them, Jenny realized, any more than you could blame a two year old who would rather play with her food than eat it. One room at a time, Jenny told herself. And one day at a time as well.

Today she'd content herself with bringing some sort of order to the first floor. Neglect had come close to killing many of the plants that filled the room. Jenny could imagine Danni's attitude: So a plant dies? Buy another. It was an attitude she didn't like, and although she was trying to avoid judging her new employer, it was hard not to.

Anne Yarwood, her lover, had taken an extraordinary amount of time and great delight in repeating all the local gossip about Danni's personal life and the reputation Danni had earned for herself both in Baysville and Boston.

Jenny thought of what a lifesaver Danni had been to her and her daughter. Danni had asked no questions, checked no references, made no demands, simply opened her home to Sara and Jenny. So what if she could write her name on any surface in the room? Where would she have gone if Danni hadn't walked into her life? To repay her, Jenny was determined to do the best job possible.

Anne and Danni had been childhood friends, Jenny had learned, though Anne claimed they'd gone their separate ways once in college. Jenny sensed from the tone in Anne's voice when she spoke about Danni that she respected this woman as much as she disliked her. Jenny wondered if Anne's feelings might be just the opposite of dislike, wondered if perhaps she'd made overtures to Danni and been rejected. There'd be no point to asking Anne — Jenny knew she was too adept at protecting her own vulnerability. She'd never admit truth that might damage herself.

Apparently, Danni had been quite a party girl in college, had openly slept around before it became fashionable. There was talk of a marriage to Garth Reynolds and a wild story about having sex with one of the waiters in the back pantry of his parents' home, which Jenny chalked up to Anne's imagination. Whatever the reason, they never married, but they still spent time together, Garth being one of a legion, according to Anne.

From Anne's gossip, Jenny had learned that Danni came from old New England stock, that there was plenty of money in the family coffers. But Danni's venture into advertising had been strictly her own doing; Anne gave her credit there. She'd begun small, worked on a few solid accounts to give her a base line of stability, and then gradually moved into the markets that involved more risk. She'd taken on accounts that none of the larger agencies were anxious to handle and designed successful campaigns for them. It wasn't long before the agency was known throughout the city.

"If she wasn't the success she is," Anne had told her the other evening, "she'd be written off as the town tramp."

"Jealous?" Jenny had asked.

"Believe me dear, we don't share the same tastes — in anything," Anne had said in a voice so cool that Jenny was suspect of her tone.

Anne could not understand why Jenny was taking the job. "Housekeepers come and go out there as regularly as the tide. You'll no sooner be settled than you'll have to leave. And what about Sara? Do you really want her a part of that scene?"

"Anne, you're not attractive when you sputter. And since when are you so concerned about Sara?"

A few moments passed before Anne had said, "Don't ever say I didn't warn you."

Warnings, Jenny thought, when did warnings ever stop me from playing a long shot?

She walked into the kitchen, took one look at the windows and decided that that was job number one. She filled a bucket with warm water and vinegar, pulled a chair over to the sink, and started cleaning, standing on tiptoe to reach for the top panes. When had these windows last been washed? Dust, grease, grime — a black film coated the glass. This is *soot,* she told herself, pure *soot.*

Intent on scrubbing the glass, she didn't realize that Duvall had come into the room until she nearly fell as he leaped toward the chair. Able to step up on the sink counter, she picked up the bucket of water and quickly doused the dog's head. She'd been generous with the vinegar, she realized, as Duvall made a howling, hasty retreat from the kitchen.

He won't try that trick with me again, she thought with satisfaction. There might be two bosses in this house, but I'll be damned if a dog's going to be one of them. She stepped down and walked into the hall where Duvall lay. As soon as he saw her, he ran upstairs, tail tucked between his legs.

"And stay up there," she called. "I'm not about to be humped by a dog. You better know it right now!"

She mopped up the water, fixed another pail, and finished the job. As she sat down to admire her work, she realized it was almost time for lunch. She wasn't sure of what she'd find in the way of staples, but a can of tuna on top of the refrigerator meant they wouldn't go hungry. There was no bread to be seen but she found a box of crackers. From the fruit she brought with her she sliced an apple and a pear, and after adding a bit of mustard and olive oil to the tuna, she called Sara. She'd already put on a kettle of water for her favorite tea.

"How do you like having lunch in our new house?" she asked Sara.

"I do. I like playing with Duvall too, Mommy. Why doesn't he come down with us? Isn't he hungry?"

Jenny smiled. "I guess not, Sara. You go up and play with him after you finish and he'll come down."

As the afternoon passed, Jenny had little trouble putting the first floor in order. Major cleaning projects she'd leave for next week, but the house was coming along just fine. While she was cutting back a collection of straggly plants, she thought about dinner. Danni hadn't said she'd be back for an evening meal, but she hadn't said she wouldn't, either. She and Sara would be having dinner — why not cook for the three of them? If Danni wasn't interested, the leftovers could be tomorrow's lunch. Jenny walked into the kitchen.

It wasn't that the pantry was bare, she laughingly told herself, just that it was stocked for a season of cocktail parties. Capers, olives, cocktail onions and pâtés had been ordered by the case. Jars of marinated artichokes, imported anchovies and smoked oysters were stacked next to tins of macadamia nuts and cashews. On a shelf of canned goods of a more ordinary nature, she saw minced clams and plum tomatoes. From a hanging wire basket she picked two onions, chopped and sautéed them, pureed the tomatoes, added garlic and spices, ground some pepper and put it all on the back burner. The clams she would prepare later, adding them to parsley, olive oil, a splash of vermouth. She found a package of linguine among boxes of foil and plastic wrap; there were French rolls in the freezer. They'd have a feast that night.

It was easy to persuade Sara to have an early dinner, even though she was still excited about being in what she already called "their" new house. Thinking about the meal she'd made, Jenny knew she wanted to share it with Danni, and she could use Sara's early dinner hour as an excuse. What adult wanted to eat at five-thirty?

It was nearly eight o'clock when Danni came home. Jenny could see that she'd had a few drinks.

"Hey, Jenny," she said, "the place looks great. What did you do to get through this disaster? Bring a bottle of uppers with you?"

Jenny watched her as she dropped her briefcase on the sofa, her jacket on a chair, and her purse on top of the TV. Danni didn't seem to notice that papers from her briefcase spilled onto the floor.

"What a day," she said. "I haven't stopped since I left this morning. You haven't either, have you? Don't feel you have to change this place overnight, Jenny."

"I can't," Jenny said with a smile. "I've made some dinner. Care to join me?"

"Love to — but I don't expect you to cook my meals. Most nights I come back just to change clothes and go out on the prowl. You'd be surprised at the variety of species I've encountered at our local watering holes. You've probably sampled some of the stock yourself. Maybe we'll both go out some night. What do you say?"

Jenny looked over at Danni. "That's not my cup of tea right now," she said.

"Suit yourself. I just don't want you to feel lonely cooped up in this place."

"We won't be lonely. Sara and I spent all last winter by ourselves at Grace Ash's place. I wanted to mention, though, that the local craft guild is looking for someone to teach a weaving class one morning a week as part of their summer program. I'd like to do it if you wouldn't mind."

"Why would I mind?" Danni said. "Sounds ideal for you. Say, whatever you've cooked smells absolutely delicious."

As she ate, Danni was surprised at how much she enjoyed having dinner with Jenny and Sara, who'd decided she'd have seconds on the linguine. The women lingered over a bottle of wine Danni had opened when she saw the meal Jenny had prepared.

"This has been like an evening at the Romagnoli's Table," Danni said. "Superb. Compliments to the chef, right Sara?"

Jenny looked at her child. "Sara, you've had a busy day. Your eyes look sleepy, very sleepy. Do you know that?"

"Can Duvall sleep in my room?"

"Sure," Danni said, "but you better hurry up. I think the sandman's already paid you a visit and sprinkled just enough sand in your eyes to keep you awake till you're tucked in bed. What do you say? Want me to go up with you?"

Holding her small hand, Danni watched Sara fall asleep. She bent over and kissed her goodnight and thought about coming home tomorrow night to this beautiful child.

While Danni was upstairs, Jenny cleared the table, stacked the dishwasher and then went into the living room where she gathered Danni's belongings together. Danni walked into the room looking much more relaxed than when she came home.

"How nice of you to go up with her," Jenny said. "She's been so happy all day — it was love at first sight for her and Duvall."

There was a moment of awkward silence between the women. During dinner, conversation had flowed so freely; now Danni felt slightly uncomfortable. She wasn't sure why. Was it the presence of Sara in her home? Was it the ease with which Jenny had assumed her responsibilities here? Was it simply the fact that her previous housekeepers had avoided both her and Duvall? Now that she thought about it, Duvall had been unusually submissive. At dinner, when Jenny had told the dog to stop begging, he obeyed, then settled at her feet. Odd.

"Well, if there's nothing else, I think I'll turn in."

"So early?" Danni asked, thinking of her own plans to go out for the evening.

"It's after eleven. That's late for me," Jenny said.

"Already? Time passed so quickly I didn't realize it."

"I hope we didn't spoil your plans for the evening," Jenny said.

"How could you have? This has been lovely. One thing about the bars in this town, they'll always be there. I think I'll turn in too. After a few minutes of paper work, that is."

Jenny stepped toward the table where she had placed Danni's briefcase and papers. "I hope you don't mind my moving these," she said.

"Not at all. In my life disorder is order, if you know what I mean. Somewhere in all of this I've convinced myself there's a method."

"I'm sure there is," Jenny said.

The two women stood only inches apart. Danni felt a tension in the air she couldn't define.

"Well, it's been quite a nice evening," she said.

"Yes it has," Jenny replied, wanting to move closer.

A few minutes later, as Jenny pulled the light quilt over her shoulders, she wondered how to reach Danni. Barriers were there, defenses. But she'd get through them. Unaccustomed to the amount of wine she had, she fell asleep with the image of Danni's sensuous mouth clear in her mind.

* * * * *

After another cigarette and a splash of brandy, Danni still felt restless. What *is* it, she asked herself. You can go out tomorrow night; there's nothing doing on Mondays anyway. She realized she wished her conversation with Jenny hadn't ended so early. She must wonder where I'm coming from asking her to take in the local pubs the way I did.

What an interesting woman, Danni mused. She smiled to herself: we're as different as night and day. Jenny had told her of growing up in a small town, the only child of a middle-aged couple, the postmaster of Library, Pennsylvania and his wife, the high school science teacher. Her mother had doted on her, as Danni could well imagine, urging her to study, to seek wider horizons for herself, to use all of her gifts and to develop others. She described a passive, reticent father who saw no reason for her to go beyond the nearby city of Pittsburgh. All that Jenny remembered of Pittsburgh, she'd said, were tall bridges spanning the three rivers and red streams of molten slag running down the hillsides from Bessemer steel furnaces that burned all night long. Her mother suggested she study in New York City and, once there, it was only a matter of time before Jenny was encouraged to try her hand at modeling to help pay her expenses. Only then, Danni reflected as she walked to her bedroom, had she and Jenny begun to share a common background.

The next day, Danni stood at the sink smoking a cigarette and drinking a cup of freshly brewed coffee. She'd forgotten how good it tasted first thing in the morning. She pulled out a stool tucked under the long butcher block counter. Sunlight filled the room as she looked at Jenny and Sara. What a perfect mother and daughter, she told herself. I should push the TV commercials again. Of course, if Jenny did go back to modeling, she wouldn't stay here —

Jenny's words broke into her thoughts. "What time will you be back?"

Danni laughed. "Not even my mother keeps tabs on me like this. But I should be home around seven. Gotta go, see you both tonight."

Impulsively, Danni leaned across the counter and kissed Sara goodbye.

Jenny walked toward the door with Danni. "Wait a minute," she said. "You don't wear your label on the outside of your blouse, do you?" She reached up and tucked the label back inside her blouse collar. For seconds, her hand remained poised in midair above Danni's shoulder. She wanted to touch her again but did not.

"Thanks," Danni said, "I'm usually more careful."

Danni wore a white linen suit, her black silk blouse revealing ample cleavage. Attaché case in hand, she looked like one of her own ads for today's successful business woman. Jenny watched her walk toward her car, a sleek silver Porsche.

A beauty, Jenny thought, just like its owner.

Before climbing into the car, Danni turned and in her smile Jenny recognized that child-like creature she'd seen when they first met.

IV

Jenny walked back inside to answer the ringing phone.
Anne's voice reminded her of the date they'd made for
lunch. She hadn't been able to locate a baby sitter, she told
Anne, but she still wanted to see her. Anne offered a solution: she'd bring a picnic lunch over to Danni's.

"Sure you want to come all the way out here?" Jenny
asked.

"It's no great drive. You forget, I grew up in Baysville.
Besides, what's nicer than love in the afternoon? And speaking of matters pertaining to romance, don't get any ideas
about the all-American heterosexual you're working for.
She's got one thing on her mind where sex is concerned,
and it involves a quaint little bit of equipment neither you
nor I happen to have."

"Are you serious?" Jenny asked, laughing lightly.

"I just don't want you getting any ideas."

"I can't believe you were never tempted to move in that direction with her."

"No way. She's not my type."

"I know your taste in women too well," Jenny teased. "Tall, blonde, beautiful — if that's not enough, Annie, she's bright, successful —"

"Not Danni Marlowe," Anne said sharply. "Let's just change the subject." Then softening her tone, she said, "I want us to enjoy the afternoon. See you in a while."

Anne arrived ahead of schedule, which surprised Jenny. Described by most people as tailored, she was tall, thin, and good looking. She wore her clothes well and enjoyed buying them, though her interest was in comfort rather than style. Today she was dressed casually in a white oxford-cloth shirt, navy slacks and clean white sneakers. Her hair was short, brushed back from her face, and the same color as her eyes which were dark brown, the lashes full and thick, the eyebrows thin arches across her forehead. There was a disarming candor in her smile which put even strangers at ease, a directness in her manner which invited confidence. She smiled easily and often, knowing how to charm her law partners and clients, her lovers as well.

"You were sweet to come out today," Jenny said.

"You're a sweet woman," Anne replied as she moved toward her. "Don't you know that yet?"

With Anne's kiss, Jenny felt not only the pleasure they had given each other over the past year, but a wave of arousal that she knew was connected to Danni. Anne's hands moved lovingly over her body; then she stepped back and looked around the room.

"This is an *enormous* place," she said. "There's plenty of room to do anything you want, isn't there?"

"I'll say. Let me show you around. She's installed

cathedral ceilings, glass sliders, skylights — yet the house still has its Victorian charm. She's very clever. Come on up and see my room."

* * * * *

Jenny had met Anne two years ago at a party given by a friend of Anne's from law school. Business brought her to New York several times a year, but that fall her trips became more and more frequent as she and Jenny began seeing each other. In a matter of weeks they became lovers. If their relationship wasn't exciting or volatile, if the sex between them wasn't wild, it was good. Neither was inclined to hold back the pleasures the other wanted and they came to know each other's body well.

From the beginning, Jenny knew not to expect more from Anne than her company and her affection. For the time being, Jenny had thought, it was enough. Feeling skeptical about the promises of romance after a short-circuited affair with a young woman architect the year before, Jenny was cautious about how much of herself she was willing to risk.

Yet it was surely more than coincidental that when she decided to return to school last year, Boston University was her first choice, and certainly more than providential that Anne found her a housesitting job in Baysville, a small, snug, seacoast town only twenty miles away.

"It's an easy commute," Anne had told her. "Rents in the city are exorbitant. If my condo wasn't so small, you could move in with me, but there's only one bedroom. Where would Sara sleep?"

There was no question in Jenny's mind that Sara came first in her life and Jenny knew that Anne wasn't all that comfortable with her daughter. She had accepted that Anne wasn't the woman she was waiting for, but she cared for Anne and valued what they *did* share. For now, Anne was the best she could have. Jenny, though, wanted permanence; she wanted another marriage. One day, she hoped, she would meet the woman who would be her partner in all that she knew was possible in a relationship.

"Isn't this a lovely room?" Jenny asked. "This spindle bed belonged to Danni's grandparents — so did the hooked rug. The design's exquisite, don't you think?" She took Anne's hand and walked to the window with her. "*Look* at the view, Annie — the surf's spectacular today! And from this very window I can have my own sunrise any morning I want it — how about that?"

"It's quite a setting," Anne pleasantly agreed.

"I knew you'd like it." Jenny looked down into the garden. Sara was brushing a patient Duvall. She motioned Anne to step away from the window. She kissed Anne, lightly at first, playfully nibbling her lips, nipping her tongue, but then Anne's attentions grew more serious. She sighed as Anne's hands moved inside her blouse, her thumbs circling Jenny's nipples. Jenny unzipped Anne's slacks, her hand grazing soft skin, slipping under silky bikini briefs.

"My, what long fingers you have," Anne whispered.

"The better to touch you with, my dear," Jenny teased, her other hand sliding down the back of Anne's slacks.

"My, what strong hands you have," Anne said, laughing lightly.

"The better to love you with, my dear," Jenny murmured.

"Then before you turn into the big, bad wolf, Grandma, let's go to bed. Little Red Riding-Hood's in the mood for a first course before lunch."

From the patio they could hear Sara calling; then the front door slammed.

Anne backed away. "Talk about timing," she said.

"Mommy, I can't find the toy we bought Duvall," Sara called. "Can you help me find it?"

Jenny quickly kissed Anne. "Don't be mad. We'll be together Thursday night." She called to Sara, "Be right down, honey."

"You know," Anne said, "I would like to see you alone now and then."

"You will, Annie. Thursday. I'm pretty sure I can leave Sara with Beth Drew."

"Why don't you leave her with Danni?" Anne asked sarcastically.

"If she's home I might suggest it," Jenny said, ignoring her tone. "The two of them seem to have really hit it off."

"As long as it's not the two of you," Anne said coolly.

"Stop pouting," Jenny said. "Let's go down and have that picnic lunch."

* * * * *

As Anne drove back to Boston, she wondered if Jenny was attracted to Danni.

Even if she is, she thought, there's no need to worry about Danni being attracted to her. If Danni were asked, she'd put lesbians in the same class as lepers, or a notch below.

Always, she thought, always I knew I was gay, even before I knew what the word meant. Always I was drawn to softness, to beauty, to women.

She saw herself and Danni when they were children, as adolescents, then as young women, friends in college — at least that first year. They had spent many free hours together those first few weeks away from home. Campus life was new to them and strange. Even though there was much to do, both felt lonely. Danni often dropped by Anne's room, sometimes suggesting they go out shopping or off campus for something to eat, but mostly wanting to talk.

Anne had spent much of her time that semester listening to Danni's stories about the different dates she had. Anne herself had made friends with a fellow from her Western Civ class and they spent so much time together that people had begun to think of them as a couple. Anne didn't think of it that way at all; he was her friend, plain and simple.

One weekend when both Danni's and Anne's roommates had gone home, Anne suggested that Danni move in until Sunday night. That Saturday evening, Danni dressed for yet another party.

She'd had her hair cut. Parted on the side, it was a straight blonde fall and just touched her shoulder. Her eyes were as clear as a blue summer sky; her lips red, full and sensuous. She brushed one side of her hair back behind her ear.

"Like it?" she asked. "Think it looks sexy this way?"

"Looks super," Anne said excitedly.

Large black baubles hung from her ears. Her blouse was black with silver threads running through it. She wore a pair of tight grey slacks.

"What do you think? These or my black ones?"

"Black," Anne said, turning over on the bed, enjoying every minute with Danni. "More sophisticated."

"Sure, for a keg party. Whatever you say. Wait a sec."

Danni stepped out of her grey slacks and sat down on the bed beside Anne.

"You're a sweet kid," Danni said. "Know that? I don't know what I'd do without you. I mean it."

"I don't either, Danni. I really don't," Anne said, her voice serious.

"You're just a big, sweet baby," she said. Danni leaned

back, her arms open wide for Anne.

Anne still remembered that embrace, remembered lying in Danni's arms for those few minutes. She remembered the rest too well. Reaching for Danni, kissing her, a hand fumbling, moving clumsily inside of her blouse. And she remembered Danni's laugh as well.

And the words: "Hey, lesbo, you're out of bounds. The territory's already claimed. You really want to make it with girls? That's sick. It freaks me out."

Danni had risen and put on the black slacks. "I better not ask you anymore how I look," she had said in a soft cruel voice, "you'll take it for a come-on." And she had walked out of Anne's room.

Anne didn't know until Sunday morning that Danni had stopped in the dorm lounge on the way to the party. Not until she went down to have breakfast at the caf the next day and the group from her wing snickered at her as she approached their table, had she realized that Danni had talked.

Past history, she told herself. Though the pain was gone, she'd never forgive her. Danni could never hurt her again yet she was uneasy at the notion of Jenny being anywhere near her . . .

The irony of Jenny working for Danni brought the real problem to mind: Sara. Just as Anne had no desire for children of her own, she had no desire for another woman's children in her life. With her, work had been her primary focus; adjusting her schedule to the needs of a young child was not something she could easily accommodate. Nor did she feel comfortable with the notion of being a surrogate parent. If she and Jenny were to live together, what would she be to Sara? A second mother? An aunt? A rival for her mother's affection?

Yet it was absurd that they weren't living together. Anne knew that they couldn't float indefinitely as they were now.

Why can't I admit what she means to me and get on with it all? She's a good woman. Who else have I met who even comes close to her?

"No one," Anne said aloud.

She thought, I'll tell her we'll start looking for an apartment whenever she wants to. In another year, she'll have her degree . . . Sara will be through first grade, not a baby anymore. I could probably find a place with a separate wing for Jenny and me.

But then again, why not wait till next year, Anne thought, once more relishing her need for privacy. As she approached a major intersection, she felt a sudden apprehension. Next year seemed very far away and at the same time much too close.

V

In a little over a month, drastic changes had taken place in Danni's life. She was aware of some of these, but others, as was characteristic of her, she ignored or chose not to recognize.

The Marlowe Agency had been geared to her lifestyle. Usually, it was mid-morning before she arrived at the office, often hung over from the night before. By 2:00 or 3:00 in the afternoon she found the pace that kept her at her desk until late in the evening. Working until 11:00 was common for Danni and her staff; married people didn't last long in her employ. In the last month, however, the Agency had become more of a 9:00 to 5:00 operation with Danni arriving early each morning to review accounts that needed her immediate attention. She had no more time for leisurely drinks

41

when the work day finally ended. Previously, Danni had enjoyed the considerable traveling that was part of running the business, but now business trips were parceled out to account executives.

Her office was located on the second floor of a town-house overlooking the Boston Common. From her desk she could look out to Beacon Street. Ignoring the steady stream of traffic below her window, she charted the passing seasons as leaves unfolded on the trees in the park, burst in an expanse of green, turned suddenly brilliant, golden, then fell in chill November, the trees to come to life again when they were trimmed with thousands of tiny blue, white, and golden lights for the holiday season.

Her account executives shared two large rooms directly behind her office; the layout, art and copy staffs comfortably occupied a suite at the rear of the building overlooking a small brick courtyard.

Mornings, Danni worked alone or met with clients, reserving the early afternoons for short meetings with her staff to review accounts and discuss strategies. Unless it was necessary, she no longer scheduled dinner or evening appointments with her clients. The attendant at the parking garage soon became accustomed to pulling her car out to the front of the lot by 6:00.

She found herself quite content to drive home directly after work each night. The thrill of seek and conquer, which had been such a driving force in her life, seemed to have diminished. Not given to introspection, she didn't think about what these changes meant.

* * * * *

Arriving home, Danni pulled into the drive, noticing that there were no bikes about. More often than not, children's bicycles were scattered in the driveway or nestled around Jenny's battered VW as Sara and her friends played in the yard. Summer showers had fallen throughout the afternoon though — not a day to be outdoors.

She skirted large puddles in the drive, then, spotting a toy in the middle of the lawn, walked through wet grass to pick it up. The gardens were all in bloom; had they ever looked lovelier? On her way to the back door, Danni remembered that her mother would be coming over tonight; she was looking forward to her visit. She smiled as she stepped into the hall. Jenny had been baking. The wonderful aroma of freshly baked bread filled the room. How much she enjoyed seeing her house transformed into a real home.

As a child, her own home life had been austere. Her father, a tall, cool, distant man, spent as little time at home as possible. Ethel Marlowe was a dynamic woman, but her energies were channeled entirely to her favorite charitable causes. Her four children weren't neglected, far from it; but Ethel did not believe in indulging them. Simple diets were best, she was convinced. When the medical profession began to proclaim the desirability of limiting the consumption of sugars and fats, she said, "I could have told them that a long time ago."

We're a no-frills family, she often told the children. As an adult, Danni realized that her mother had gone too far with her philosophy. Dinner time, in Danni's memory, was the most dismal hour of the day.

Now there was something magical about dinner, about the pleasure and imagination Jenny took in concocting so wide a variety of meals that Danni believed Jenny had yet to repeat a menu. Even if she had made the dish before, she varied it by adding some new spice or ingredient.

As Danni walked into the room, Sara ran to her. "Look how clean and soft my hair is, Danni. Mommy washed it with rainwater and we've got lots and lots left. Want Mommy to wash your hair, Danni?" she asked, the towel still wrapped around her neck.

"Sara," Danni said, "I have my hair washed at Antoine's. Don't you remember we visited him last week? He told you how pretty your hair was."

"I know. I remember. But it's fun having your hair washed with rainwater."

Jenny, looking cool and pretty in navy shorts and a kelly green halter, greeted her with a smile. "I don't mind washing it for you if you like, Danni," she said.

Danni decided to indulge Sara and join the party. She unbuttoned the cuffs of her lemon silk blouse and slipped it off.

Jenny gazed at Danni's shoulders and long, graceful arms. Her flesh was tight. Her breasts filled the lace, snap-front bra she wore. Transfixed, Jenny watched Danni drape the blouse over the back of a chair and casually reach for a thick, peach terry cloth towel which she wrapped around her shoulders.

Danni walked toward Jenny; their bodies brushed as they moved to the sink and Jenny felt as if she'd been touched by fire.

"Now no soap in my eyes, okay?" Danni teased.

"I'm a pro," Jenny said, wanting to calm her feelings. "Right, Sara?"

As she poured the soft rainwater through Danni's hair, Jenny tried to relax. "Could you move closer to the sink?" she asked.

Danni obliged; Jenny massaged Danni's scalp vigorously, her breasts lightly touching Danni's supple back. Feeling her flesh so close to Danni's, her nipples stiffened inside her flimsy halter. She savored the moment, not wanting to stop or move away from the other woman.

Sara interrupted the spell. "I want to pour some water over Danni's head," she said. "Can I, Mommy?"

"Sure, baby, we're almost ready to begin rinsing."

Danni was enjoying the whole procedure. Jenny's touch was soothing, no doubt about it. It was strange, feeling her body so close.

Jenny began the final rinse, then wrapped a thick towel around Danni's head, tucking the ends in turban style.

As she brushed drops of water from her cheeks, Danni turned and said, "Thank you. That felt wonderful."

"You're welcome," Jenny said. Their eyes met. More than ever, she wanted to comprehend what was behind Danni's cool, clear gaze. This evening, for the first time, she felt a subtle power in her eyes, as if Danni was savoring the moment through the exchange they now shared.

The mood was interrupted by Sara's laughter. "I told you rainwater was special, Danni."

As Danni smiled at Sara and Jenny, she reflected on their presence in her home. Jenny was not just another employee, Danni realized, but her friend. She hadn't had close friends when she was growing up, but with Jenny in her life she was beginning to understand what she'd missed.

Danni lit a cigarette. "You know, Jenny, you and Sara have made life very nice for me. I appreciate all the things you do that aren't part of the job."

Jenny smiled. She knew Danni liked her; they had grown close as the weeks of the summer had passed. She also knew that if she over-reacted, if she made any wrong moves, she could lose Danni's friendship and affection. She looked at Danni, wanting to connect again in the way they had only seconds before.

"You're happy here, I hope," Danni asked.

"Of course we are."

"I'm glad." Danni slipped into her blouse and rubbed the towel still wrapped around her head. "Hey, I took a look at the calendar today," she said, her voice casual, chatty. "You know Labor Day is only six weeks off?"

"Don't I ever," Jenny replied, knowing that the mood

was broken. "I've got to register for courses next week —"

"Before you hit the books," Danni interrupted, "we're going to give the summer a big send-off. I do it every year — it's my annual Labor Day weekend party. I'd like you there as my guest." She added, "Why don't you bring that mysterious friend you see on your nights off?" Then Danni raised her hand before Jenny could respond. "Tell you what. I'll get you a date. I've got just the fellow in mind."

"Maybe I'd just as soon come alone," Jenny said, and laughed.

"Oh come on. Trust me. No one's ever faulted my taste in men." Undoing the turban, Danni rubbed her hair with the thick towel and smiled at Sara. "Honey, you have wonderful ideas. What do you think, Jenny? Is there time for Sara and me to go off for some ice cream before my mother arrives?"

"Ice cream before dinner?"

"Never," Danni said. "We'll bring it back for dessert. I'm in the mood for something sweet. All I need is a few minutes with the blow dryer and I'll be ready. What do you say, Sara? Want to pick out the flavors?"

Just then, Ethel Marlowe tapped at the back door, pushed it open and stepped into the kitchen.

She was gentry, Jenny thought, no doubt about it. This tall, stately woman in her winter years naturally commanded attention.

"Hello, Mother," Danni said, giving her the customary kiss on both cheeks.

Ethel smiled at her youngest child. Danni had always been her favorite. Independent, determined to go her own way, high-spirited and clever, she didn't get along with the rest of the family. Years ago, she'd told Ethel that she refused to spend any more time than necessary in a house of dullards. Secretly, Ethel agreed with Danni's estimation of her siblings. They were her husband's children: cold, distant, conventional. Danni was hers. Ethel was proud of the success Danni had made of her agency. She knew of Danni's personal reputation, but she was confident that this would change. Danni might be a cross for the rest of the family to bear but not for her. She knew that Danni, with her strong will and intelligence, would someday understand the streak of restlessness in herself. With this insight, she would be able to tame it — and one day find love.

Ethel Marlowe, she admitted only privately, was no saint herself. The survivor of a loveless marriage, she saw her own life as a series of compromises not always made for the best reasons. True, there was never public scandal attached to her name. True, she had stood by her husband and raised four children to adulthood. True, she was a welcome guest at any home in the community. But only because of impeccable discretion.

She had been nearly forty before succumbing to temptation. On a trip to Greece she met an Athenian lawyer nearly ten years younger than she. There was never any question whether she and Nikos would see each other or even correspond after the end of her journey. The following year, on a cruise of the Caribbean islands, she found it quite natural to strike up a friendship with a retired archeology professor. He did want to see her again, but she declined.

With the passing years, opportunities presented themselves to Ethel Marlowe; she rarely rejected them. Perhaps she didn't match her youngest daughter's appetite for sensual pleasures, but she had curiosity and imagination, along with the time and money to indulge both. She had also developed a tolerance which came from having lived her own life without love for so long. She knew that those who found it were fortunate wherever or however it came their way.

"Mother," Danni said, "I promised to take Sara to Regina's for ice cream. Want to come?"

"No, dear, I think I'll relax and visit with Jenny."

As Danni and Sara closed the door behind them, Ethel looked at Jenny and thought, My lord, she really is a beauty. Jenny, seated across the room, was somewhat intimidated by Ethel. She felt nervous with her, awkward, perhaps because she'd never been alone with her.

"Mrs. Marlowe, can I get you something?"

"My dear, I do wish you'd call me Ethel. And, yes, bourbon on the rocks, if you'll join me."

Jenny poured the amber-red bourbon over the clear ice cubes, and a white wine with seltzer for herself. She sat on the sofa beside Ethel, placing the drinks on the dark gleaming coffee table.

"Jenny," Ethel said, "I'm glad we have this chance to be alone for a few minutes. I've been wanting to chat with you."

Jenny tensed. Ethel Marlowe might be doing her best to seem casual and relaxed but to Jenny she was formidable.

"I'm a very direct person," she continued, "especially where my daughter is concerned. First, I want to say that the changes in Danni's life since you've arrived have been wondrous. You and your daughter have made a home for my child. I can't express the delight and pleasure this gives me. Danni's not getting younger and I've felt for some time that she'd have to slow her pace. Garth, of course, has been a strong positive influence, but aside from him, I don't think there's anyone who's meant terribly much to her. Whatever charms you and Sara are casting over my daughter, believe me, I approve."

Jenny found herself drinking her wine faster than usual. When she looked at Ethel's glass, she realized she needed a refill, too. She walked to the bar.

Ethel continued, "I feel that you see what a sensitive woman my daughter is, that you understand that side of her nature that is, well, perhaps child-like. When this side of her nature is nurtured, she's capable of great things. When it's ignored, she tends to be wild, self-indulgent, and all those other adjectives our kind fellow townspeople have applied to her. But I know one thing about her that she herself doesn't know: she needs someone to take care of her. I'm concerned, naturally, about who she'll have after I'm gone."

"She'll always have Garth, Mrs. Marlowe," Jenny managed to say. "He'll always be there for her."

"As friends, yes. He and Danni will always be close. But Garth has a demanding profession and his own life to live. Perhaps you don't know this — after their engagement was broken, he married a young internist. Liz was wonderful in many ways. But the marriage failed. Garth so wanted a family; he still does. Liz had no desire for children. She married a man who shares her feelings about this, and from what I've heard they're both quite happy. Garth deserves *his* happiness. He'll move on; he'll find what he needs from life."

This time, Jenny didn't touch her glass. She listened to Ethel's words as she looked out on the evening sky.

"I've lived many years. I'm not naive. Which brings us to you, Jenny. You're an exceptional woman, obviously capable of making choices for yourself, which few people are. Danni's told me of your modeling career in New York. That doesn't surprise me — you are, my dear, beautiful. But I admire the strength it took to recognize you had to find other avenues in your life. I don't know, of course, the details of your marriage, but intuition tells me you were the stronger partner. Just like your modeling career, it took strength to walk away from a situation that was untenable, a strength that perhaps I didn't have in my own marriage. You value your relationship with your daughter, that's obvious. But you haven't compromised that either, have you? Do you know what I'm talking about, Jenny?"

"I think I do," Jenny said, realizing that this was a wise, perceptive woman. She turned to meet her steady gaze.

Ethel continued, "You know, one of the benefits of age

is that you develop a sense of history, a sense of the past, even if the past involves nothing more than knowing the people who live around you. I've known Anne Yarwood, for example, since she was a child. I know, of course, that Anne is a lesbian. She's discreet, but it's part of her general nature to be discreet. That's probably one of the reasons she's done so well in her profession. It would be hard to find a more reliable lawyer than Anne, or in many ways a nicer person.

"As I say," Ethel continued, "I've known her all her life. She and Danni went off to college together. I always felt that Anne chose the school because of the crush she had on Danni. Schoolgirl crushes are nothing new, of course.

"At any rate, Danni was oblivious to the whole thing, and now that I think back on it, she was rather insensitive when Anne very courageously revealed her feelings. Danni's rejection was cruel; I don't think Anne's ever forgiven her."

"I didn't know any of this," Jenny said softly. Stunned by Ethel's revelation, she now understood Anne's animosity. "I knew Anne had a grudge against Danni, but not what was behind it."

"Do you see what I mean about history?" Ethel smiled kindly. "I learned this all many years later, from a cherished friend of mine, Norma Potter." Ethel waited for Jenny's response.

"Norma Potter," Jenny repeated. "Yes, Anne and I had dinner with her —"

"And Lucille," Ethel said, gently interrupting. "Her lover."

Momentarily taken aback by the comfortable way Ethel used the phrase, Jenny repeated, "And Lucille."

"I hope you're not upset that Norma spoke so directly about your relationship with Anne. Directness has always been one of her virtues.

"In many ways Norma reminds me of Danni — in her bad ways as well as her good, unfortunately. I suppose I know Norma Potter as well as I know anyone. When she was younger, she was very similar to Danni. Drank too much and lived in a turmoil that perhaps only she understood. If she did.

"It was sad, Jenny. She was not able to find any measure of happiness in her life. I'm not sure she had any idea of what she was looking for until she found it."

Ethel sipped her drink. "Do you know her whole story? She contracted hepatitis when she was still in her thirties. Just as she was on the verge of regaining her health, she started drinking again. Suicide, pure and simple, if she didn't stop. She ended up in the hospital again. Thank God — that's when she met Lucille. It wasn't only her nursing skills. . . . From then on, Norma's life began to change. No doubt about it, Lucille saved her life. I've sometimes feared that Danni's on a similar path. She has her work — but that's not enough."

Jenny was confused. What did this have to do with her relationship with Anne? Ethel saw Norma and Lucille as worthy human beings — in that light, she gave tacit approval to her relationship with Anne.

Jenny looked up. "And so what you're saying is, you know that Anne and I are lovers and you don't disapprove of my working for your daughter."

"No, Jenny, that's not what I'm saying." Ethel paused for a moment before continuing. "What I'm saying is, I believe you care deeply for my daughter. Am I right?"

Jenny hesitated and then her voice but a whisper said, "Yes. I do."

"Does she know how much she means to you?"

"I don't think so."

"Does she know about you and Anne?"

Jenny shook her head. "That would be the furthest thought from her mind."

"When are you going to tell her?"

"I don't know. Right now I'm confused about the relationship myself. Anne and I mean a great deal to each other. I moved to Baysville because of her. She's one of the few friends I have here. And yet —" Jenny couldn't finish the sentence.

"I think you should tell Danni soon," Ethel said encouragingly. "This is a small town. Danni will find out about the two of you one of these days. She won't take too easily to the idea if she hears it from someone else."

"I think you're probably right."

"You know, Jenny, for whatever reasons, sad as they may be, my daughter has never truly loved. Should she come to love you, as unconventional as it may still be, I would accept it. I've known for too many years what it is to live without love, and how gracious a gift it is when it comes."

Ethel reached out and took the younger woman's hand. Jenny felt her warmth and admired her for her kindness and her honesty.

"You may be shocked by what I've just said," Ethel continued, "but you must realize how very shocked I am by what appears to be the complete turn-around in my daughter's life. She's not permitted anyone to come as close to her as she has you. You weren't aware of that were you?"

"No. Danni's so very private about what seems meaningful to her. She banters, makes jokes, flip comments, but we haven't talked about anything — or anyone — that's important."

"That doesn't surprise me at all. But the time will come when you will." Ethel smiled and raised an empty glass. "I wonder, Jenny, if Danni and I are going to have our game of Scrabble tonight."

"They'll be back soon," Jenny said reassuring her with a smile.

As Jenny made another drink for Ethel, Danni and Sara

walked into the room. Jenny looked at Danni. Her hair was soft, wavy, casually brushed back from her face. She seemed relaxed and happy. It was obvious to Jenny that Ethel approved of Danni's new hairstyle. Sara ran over to Jenny, chocolate sauce on her chin and the collar of her shirt.

"Sara, have you had a sundae before dinner?"

"It was *good,* Mommy. I had chocolate and marshmallows and nuts and cherries — hey, how did you know?"

"Come on, Jenny," Danni said, falling into a chair, "don't you think this new hairdo deserves one of Regina's specials? Sara, weren't you going to put the ice cream in the freezer for me? Remember, they have to guess the flavors we bought."

* * * * *

It was late that evening when Ethel walked toward the front door with the two women.

"Mother," Danni said, "you could let me win a game now and then out of family loyalty if nothing else."

"Danni, by now you should know I play to win. And I think you do too, my dear," she said, turning to Jenny.

"I try," Jenny replied, "but gamblers have to take chances."

"Taking chances makes life interesting." Ethel bid them both goodnight.

Later, as Danni sat at her desk writing a few short memos she'd intended to finish before leaving the office, Jenny thought of Ethel's words. She felt in the mood to gamble, ready to take a chance.

She walked over to the desk and stood behind Danni. She reached out and put her hands on Danni's shoulders, massaging the back of her neck.

"Feels good," Danni said. "Don't stop."

But Jenny did stop, sensing that this wasn't the right time.

I can't lose her now, she thought, not when she's so close.

Impulsively, she leaned over and lightly kissed the top of Danni's head. "Your hair smells so fresh," she said.

Danni turned, gave her a quick smile. "Thanks for the shampoo."

VI

Danni, Garth, Jenny and Sara were spending the day on Danni's sailboat, the *Interlude*. They'd dropped anchor off Peddocks Island, one of the many small dots of land in the coastal waters off their south shore town. Over the past six weeks, they'd spent most of their weekend afternoons on the boat, sailing much of the day, circling the islands that lay beyond the harbor channel, crossing the waters in a pattern that wove lazy eights through the swells.

They had no interest in sailing the open sea; the islands afforded protection that was comforting and familiar. Sara liked Hog Island because of its name. Jenny liked Grape Island in Hingham Bay. Garth liked the challenge of sailing the narrow channels between Gallops and Lovell Islands; Danni felt at home cruising around Bumkin. They towed

the dinghy so that they could row to one of the small islands
for lunch or a swim if they felt like it. At low tide most of
the islands had small beaches where Sara could hunt for
periwinkles and hermit crabs. They often collected mussels
for a late afternoon snack at Danni's, steaming them in white
wine and a trace of garlic.

On days when the sailing had been especially exhilarating,
Danni would ask Garth to open a bottle of champagne. On
lazy afternoons, she'd choose white wine and Jenny might
bring out smoked salmon or oysters or a more exotic treat
such as lobster mousse.

Today, as always, Jenny had brought a lunch; they
feasted on fruit and cheese, sliced turkey and ham, iced tea
and bottles of cold beer. Afterward they were all content
to relax in the sun, watching sails flutter in the wind, while
Sara counted jelly fish swimming by.

Danni sat with a knee up, her back against the cabin,
watching Jenny doze in the sun, her head cradled in the arm
folded above her head. How nicely she's tanned, Danni
thought. Then she noticed the short tufts of hair under her
arms — auburn, soft and curly, glistening in the sun. Usually,
Danni didn't care for this look on women, but with Jenny
she rather liked it. Danni smiled — in fact, she couldn't think
of a single thing about Jenny that she didn't like. How
quickly their friendship had grown — how much she enjoyed
Jenny's company — even her affection. Danni herself had
never been openly affectionate. Even with her many lovers,
she would not have described herself as warm. And she had
certainly never been easy in her affections with a woman
before, not even her mother.

With Jenny it was different. Danni basked in her warm
touches. Often it was she herself who reached out to touch
Jenny to emphasize a point or to encourage Jenny in what
she was saying. It felt safe and natural to touch her — and
sweet. This was the kind of friendship European women

have, Danni told herself, or women in Latin American countries. It was a lack in our own culture that any kind of physical contact between friends of the same sex was frowned upon. . . .

Sitting on the *Interlude* that sunny afternoon, Danni thought of all that Jenny had told her about her modeling career, her marriage, her decision to leave her husband and move away from New York. There was only one subject she didn't discuss, Danni mused, and that was the identity of her lover. Why was Jenny so reticent, so evasive of her questions? And who was this mystery lover? Twice a week she went out, Tuesday and Thursday, sometimes not returning until morning, although lately she was coming back earlier and earlier.

Danni knew Jenny would explain her personal situation if asked, but for reasons not entirely clear to her, she felt apprehensive about inquiring. Perhaps Jenny was seeing a married man who somehow managed to be free two nights of the week. Danni hoped so; even though she knew it was selfish of her, she didn't want anyone taking Jenny and Sara out of her life. Jenny was so desirable, though — why weren't there other men who claimed her time? It was all a mystery, but she knew she wasn't working very hard to solve it. Why should she? What could be more pleasant than this?

As if Jenny could read her thoughts, she slowly opened her eyes, pale green in the bright sunlight, and focused them on Danni.

"Nice nap?" Danni asked softly.

"Hmmmmm," Jenny answered, sitting up and stretching. She smiled. She was framed by the sun, a pale, golden disc in the afternoon sky.

They sat several feet apart, but it seemed to Danni that there was no distance between them. An illusion caused by the light, Danni thought, knowing that she wanted Jenny even closer.

As if answering the wish, Jenny moved over beside her. "How are we doing?" she asked.

"We're doing fine," Danni answered with a smile.

In a casual gesture, Jenny reached over and rested her hand on Danni's leg, patting her knee. "Good," she said.

As her hand gently grazed Danni's thigh, Danni felt a sweet sensation sweep her body. Unsettled by Jenny's touch, she quickly turned toward the bow.

"Garth," she said, "have you and Sara got enough fish for the day?"

Garth was stretched out on the deck. The drop line he held in his hand trailed behind him in the water. "Enough for the cat," he said lazily. "Why?"

"Because I'd like to set sail. I don't want to risk having to use the running lights."

He sat up and pulled in his line. "Let me pull up the anchor."

"Be right up to help," she said.

* * * * *

Jenny loved to watch Danni work. She was truly the captain of her boat.

Jenny had known little about sailing before she met Danni, but over the summer she'd become a good first mate. It was Garth's turn to assist Danni today, and while he and Danni pulled up the anchor, Jenny called Sara to sit beside her. There wasn't room or need for a third person at the bow, and Jenny did her part by staying out of the way and making sure that Sara wasn't underfoot.

She liked sailing with Danni; the four of them had become a team. Yet she often wished for another opportunity to sail alone with Danni such as that Sunday when Garth was out of town. Jenny had arranged for Sara to spend the day with Beth, and the two of them were free to sail. It wasn't a particularly eventful day, Jenny remembered, with little wind and slow sailing. Even the sun had hidden behind a curtain of grey mist. For the better part of an hour, they had bobbed about waiting for a wind to come up, but it was obvious that this wasn't a sailor's sea.

"This must be boring for you," Danni had said, adjusting the jib line.

"No, not at all. The sky and the sea are almost the same color today. Makes me wish I could paint. I'd call it a study in grey."

"Why don't you give it a try?" Danni had asked. "There's an easel somewhere in the attic, I'm sure."

"Don't think so. I've been working on a design for a weaving I'd like to begin next week. I don't want to find any convenient distractions for myself."

"All right. Just as you say," Danni had said. "I like the way you make choices for yourself, Jenny. I've always been too adept at inventing excuses whenever I feel like postponing something or getting myself off the hook. . . ."

Now, as Jenny stretched out, a folded sweatshirt a pillow for her head, she watched Danni, feeling the closeness of that afternoon – this afternoon as well. She longed to touch her but contented herself instead with the sight of Danni gazing out at the horizon.

Danni was letting her hair grow longer and she'd pulled it back with a scarf, accenting the lines of her face, the height of her forehead, the breadth of her cheeks. She looked Scandinavian, as if she'd been born in a Danish fishing village or on a farm in Norway. She wore no makeup, not even lipstick, and she needed none; the salt air seemed to do wonders for her skin. Her levis, the blue denim bleached almost to grey, were tight and worn; the white duck-cloth sailing shirt and dark brown boat shoes had given many summers of comfortable wear. It was the kind of outfit hard to imagine anyone ever throwing away. From time to time, she absently inhaled on her cigarette. She seems so at home here, Jenny thought; this is her world, where she belongs.

Jenny could feel desire so strongly in her own body that she felt it difficult to believe that Danni was sharing none of it. But she'd fallen victim to that illusion before, Jenny thought, remembering.

She'd developed a strong, quick friendship with Sara's first nursery school teacher, Leslie, a bright, vibrant woman with boundless energy. When Jenny had told her of her interest in art during an after-school conversation, Leslie invited Jenny to the opening of a new gallery on 73rd Street. Bubbly and friendly, fun to be with, Leslie had seemed to like her very much — and Jenny certainly liked her. They began going to dinner and the movies on Friday nights; sometimes Leslie dropped by Jenny's apartment on Saturday or Sunday afternoons.

One night, relaxing in a small café, Jenny impulsively took Leslie's hand in her own. She did this in the guise of reading Leslie's palm, but as she held the woman's hand in her own, what had seemed a harmless, silly game grew serious. Still new to gay life, her first lesbian experience had happened so naturally that she expected future encounters to be the same, especially this one. But Leslie was embarrassed by Jenny's sudden intensity.

"You like women, don't you?" she asked.

"Don't you?" Jenny replied, stroking her fingers, the palm of her hand.

"No," Leslie said, abruptly pulling her hand away, "not in that way. Why would you think I do?"

Jenny felt as if a glass of cold water had been splashed in her face.

"I don't know," she said, confused and embarrassed. "I'm so fond of you, Leslie."

"Yes. I'm fond of you, too. But as a friend."

After that, there had been other rejections, not quite so painful, when she'd mistaken friendship for physical attraction. Much as she wanted Danni, she didn't want to risk that rejection now.

Jenny turned her face to the wind; it was from the southeast and would bring them swiftly home. No fear of returning after dark — with this wind, they'd be at their mooring in record time.

* * * * *

With Danni at the tiller, Garth sat opposite Jenny and Sara. A brisk trip, he thought; it wouldn't be long before he'd be letting down the sails.

This was perfect relaxation, he reflected contentedly. Once on the boat, whether he was sailing, stretched out on the deck, or fishing with Sara, problems at the hospital and elsewhere vanished. Danni, Jenny and Sara — this was what was missing in his life. A family.

But how long would it be before Jenny would think about another permanent relationship with a man? Danni had told him that Jenny had a steady two nights a week affair which hadn't shown signs of developing into anything more serious. Maybe Jenny was still nursing the wounds of her marriage. She'll make some lucky man a lovely wife, he thought — but not him. Who are you kidding, he asked himself. If she wasn't quickly turning into Danni's right hand man — or woman — you'd ask her out in a minute. His relationship with Danni was delicately balanced; he didn't want to chance jeopardizing it. Besides, in a strange way, he liked things the way they were.

He looked at Jenny relaxing in the sun and Danni working the tiller. Sunlight glimmered through Jenny's thick auburn hair, highlighting the tones of deep red and rich brown; sea breezes blew Danni's blonde tresses back from her face, salt spray splashing lightly across the deck in the wake of the *Interlude's* homeward sail. Jenny was obviously content with the life she was living and Danni had never looked happier. For all of Danni's independence and strength, she was flourishing from Jenny's attention. Clearly, she needed someone to look after her. He felt a tinge of jealousy that she had never allowed him to care for her in this way.

Ahead was the harbor and the marina; behind him the open sea reflected the strong afternoon sun as the boat cut through the waves. Watching the patterns made by the sun and water, he stopped thinking about it all. Feeling the warmth of the sun on his body, he felt relaxed, at peace. What else mattered? He decided not to ponder the present situation.

VII

Soon, Sara informed Danni, she'd be six years old, and on her birthday her mother always let her have anything she wanted.

"Anything?"

"Yes. Anything I want. Like waffles or hot dogs or pizza. Whatever I like best I get. Then I get a birthday cake and presents and ice cream."

Danni thought about what she'd buy for Sara. She started with a swing set, then Jenny stated that one gift was enough, especially since she knew how expensive it was. Danni was disappointed; she wanted to do more. At least Sara's birthday fell on a Sunday and they could all be together that day. She knew the perfect place to take mother and daughter.

The day itself promised to be bright and sunny. Both

women sang Happy Birthday to Sara when she ran into the kitchen that morning. Excitedly, she opened her presents, squealing when she opened the paint set sent by her father, and the bright red record player from her mother.

Danni had tied a yellow ribbon around the large cardboard box in the garage. Sara was thrilled when she found out what it was. Danni promised her that she and Jenny would put the swing set together very soon. They climbed in Jenny's car and drove over to pick up Beth and five-year-old Stephen.

Jenny's friend Beth lived on the first floor of a brick townhouse near Baysville's town square. Often they would walk from the apartment to the center where Jenny enjoyed the activity generated by the many shops and restaurants. Along the way, the narrow, winding streets took them past the town library, the elementary school and the once thriving boot factory, now an expensive condominium complex.

Located a few towns away from Baysville, the amusement park rose like a cotton candy city on the edge of the sea. Both kids shrieked with excitement when they saw the roller coaster. Beth and Jenny just looked at each other.

Danni said, "When I was a kid I so wanted to come here. My mother had a fit about the whole idea. But an aunt from New Jersey brought me once. I never forgot it. I loved the rides — the faster and higher the better. The roller coaster was my favorite."

"I'm afraid to go on rides like that," Beth said. "I don't feel they're mechanically safe."

"Jenny, looks like you're the lucky one," Danni said with a laugh.

She was terrified by heights. Going on that ride was the last thing Jenny wanted to do. The track, with its twists and curves, looked as flimsy as if it had been constructed from popsicle sticks. Not wanting to spoil Danni's fun though, she smiled and said, "Sure."

Jenny breathed a sigh of relief as the kids' excitement took Danni's attention away from the roller coaster. Maybe they would keep Danni too busy, maybe she would forget the ride.

Each child picked a favorite horse on the merry-go-round and rode the magic circle once, twice, then three times. Only Danni's promise to take them both on the ferris wheel persuaded them to leave.

Jenny and Beth watched the bright orange and gold striped car move upwards to the top of the arch. The children sat perfectly still, each clutching the guard rail with one hand, and Danni's hand with the other. At the top the car swung back and forth in what must have seemed like the middle of the sky to Sara and Stephen. Bravely, Sara ventured a wave; Stephen never moved. The car inched its way back to earth; as soon as the attendant raised the guard rails, the children ran happily to their mothers.

Feasting on cotton candy, hot dogs, fried dough, pizza, slush and popcorn, they walked from one end of the park to the other, spending dimes on games of fish and toss-a-ring, quarters on photos from an ancient automatic camera, dollars on strips of tickets that the kids quickly converted into rides. Outside the white picket fences of Kiddie-Land were long green-slatted park benches. Gratefully, Jenny and Beth walked toward one as Danni led Sara and Stephen to the Drive-a-Car ride. The two women watched her giving the kids careful instructions.

Beth turned to Jenny. "I would never picture Danni the way she is today. She gives the impression of being so cool and sophisticated, but she's really like a big kid, don't you think? I've just heard so many stories about her that I can't believe she's the same person. Is she really as wild as they say?"

"Wild? I don't think so. I think she's a very nice woman, a very special woman."

"Does she know about you and Anne?"

"Why should she?"

"The two of you seem pretty tight, if you ask me."

"We're just friends."

Danni walked over to the bench and sat down between the two. "Well, they're having the time of their lives," she said. "Whew, I need to take a little break myself."

They all watched Stephen and Sara aim their rubber bumpered cars at each other. "Great ride for getting rid of aggressions," Danni said.

The kids soon ran over, out of breath and happy.

"Come on, Jenny," Danni said. "Let's take that train ride in the sky."

Danni was having such a good time, how could Jenny refuse? They took their seats in the first car — Danni's idea. The car started the slow climb up the tracks.

Danni turned to Jenny and smiled. "Fun, huh? Hey, when we get to the top, look in the direction of the parking lot and see if your car's still there."

Jenny had no chance to answer; they'd begun the down-hill plunge. Frozen in her seat, she closed her eyes — then kept them open — it didn't matter. Up and down they raced the track, cars swinging wildly around sharp curves, shrill, excited laughter piercing the air until the ride came to its sudden halt.

Danni hopped out of the car. "God, I've never heard anyone scream the way you did."

Jenny got up slowly. She was shaking. Her stomach felt as if it were still on the moving roller coaster. Danni's smile vanished at the sick look on Jenny's face, her sallow complexion. "Are you okay?"

"No. I think I'm going to be sick."

"Can you make it to the rest room?"

Jenny nodded.

"I'll have Beth and the kids wait for us at the car."

When Danni returned, Jenny was leaning over the sink washing her face.

"Feeling any better?" Danni asked.

"A little. I just wish I hadn't eaten so much." She held onto the edge of the sink for support.

Worried by her paleness, Danni took a few paper towels, moistened them with warm water, wiped Jenny's face. She took the sweater from around her own shoulders and wrapped Jenny in it.

Danni said, "You told me you didn't like life in the fast lane. I should have listened." She put her arm around Jenny's shoulder and helped her to the car.

"Mommy," Sara said in alarm.

"She's okay, Sara, but let Mommy get in the back seat and close her eyes while we drive home. And you and Stephen be nice and quiet for a while."

When they dropped Beth off, she said, "I'll call tomorrow and see how you are."

Jenny nodded and managed a smile.

Driving home, they made their way through outer Baysville, with its large white Federal homes set back from the wide tree-lined avenue. Quickly Danni drove out of town and toward the coast.

"I'll have you home in a minute," she said with concern.

Later, after tucking Sara under the covers, Danni looked in on Jenny. She sat down on the side of the bed. "I'm sorry you feel so sick. We didn't have to take that ride."

"I wanted to. We were all having such a good time."

"Well, next time we'll stay on the ground. You're a gutsy lady — know that?" Danni brushed the top of Jenny's hair back from her forehead. "Turn over — I'll give you a nice back rub. Guaranteed to lull you to sleep in seconds."

Danni began a slow and deep massage. Jenny, her head cradled in her arms, could feel her back muscles relax, then her whole body. How gentle and sensitive Danni could be.

There are so many sides to her, she thought, drifting off to sleep. I want to know them all. How lovely to have her near. . . .

VIII

A few days later, on a sunny, balmy afternoon, Danni decided to stop off at The Mooring for a drink. Choosing a section of the bar that overlooked the harbor, she pulled out a stool and ordered a gin and tonic. The quinine was fresh and bubbly; the wedge of lime tart and sour, yet she could still taste the clean flavor of the gin. She reached for cigarettes and thought, It feels good to unwind. I like this place — it's always too long between visits.

An hour later she walked from the parking lot back inside the restaurant and dialed her own number from a pay phone.

"Jenny? It's me. I'm at The Mooring. I've got car trouble. The auto club's here — it's the electrical system, they'll have to tow it to the dealer. Any chance of you coming down to get me?"

"Sure, I was just about to take Sara over to have supper with Stephen. I'm sure Beth won't mind if I drop Sara off and head on down your way. Be there as soon as I can."

Danni had finished her third drink of the early evening when she saw Jenny walking toward her, a large tote bag slung casually over her shoulder. She wore white linen slacks, a black sleeveless top.

Danni, feeling slightly tipsy, called out, "Hi — come on over and have a drink."

Jenny stepped up to the bar and sat down next to her. "What are you drinking?"

"Gin and tonic. Best drink in the world on a day like this — best place in the world to drink one. Or two. Or three. Look at this view. Ever seen a prettier harbor?"

Jenny smiled at Danni's slightly exaggerated gestures. "It's a beautiful harbor, Danni. And," she added, looking around, "it's a lovely restaurant."

"No place like The Mooring, Jen. I've been coming here all my life, know that? What do you say we stay for dinner?"

"I'd like to," Jenny said.

Danni took out a cigarette and reached for the matches down the bar. Jenny picked them up and handed them to her but Danni held the cigarette between her lips, gesturing for Jenny to light it. As she struck the match, Jenny wondered how long Danni had been here before she called.

"A lady always likes to have her cigarette lighted, my dear," Danni said, in a tone that mocked the formality she mimicked.

"Of course, of course," Jenny said, putting the book of matches in Danni's hand, allowing her fingers to linger on her cool, soft skin.

The drinks arrived. Danni picked hers up. "Did you know that Garth and I had one of our engagement parties here? Did you know the two of us were going to get married a century and a half ago?"

"I'd heard that," Jenny said, stirring her drink.

"Yep. We were. Till his mother caught me in her pantry fucking one of the waiters. It's so bizarre no one would believe it. Just so happens it's true. So what? It's past history, right?"

"If you say so," Jenny said.

"Well, I do." Danni gave Jenny a long look, as if she were having a hard time focusing. "You were a real pal to come down here and rescue me." She reached out and brushed Jenny's hair back from her face. "You're beautiful, Jenny," she said, "so beautiful."

"So are you," Jenny said, looking directly into Danni's eyes.

"But I was never a model. You were. You could still be working if you wanted to be. How could you ever give it up?"

Jenny shrugged. "How could you ever fuck a waiter in somebody's pantry?"

"Good point."

Danni turned back to the view, and whether she was spellbound by sails billowing in the wind or feeling slightly buzzed, Jenny wasn't sure. Probably the latter. As they sat at the bar, their knees touched. Did Danni feel the same surge of pleasure from their touch that she did? She wanted to touch Danni, to hold her, to let her know all the things she meant to her. She placed her arm over the back of Danni's stool; her hand grazed the supple line of her back.

As if she'd been tickled or shocked, Danni sat up straight, then turned to Jenny and smiled. She propped her elbow on the bar and rested her head in her open palm.

"How about if we get some air?" Jenny asked. "Let's take a walk along the beach."

"Okay. Then we'll have dinner, pick up Sara, head on

home and worry about the car in the morning. Fair enough?"

"Sure," Jenny said.

Danni pulled out a fistful of bills and left a few on the bar. "Let's take that walk," she said, heading for the door.

As they stepped onto the sand, Danni struggled to keep her balance.

Laughing, Jenny said, "Take your shoes off."

"Good idea," Danni agreed. "You've got lots of good ideas, Jenny. Know that?"

"I don't know about that, but there's a reason not too many people wear high heels on the beach."

"You've got *plenty* of good ideas, and I don't mean just about those shoes."

Danni sat in the sand and kicked off her heels. Jenny sat down next to her, thinking, She's fun like this; her defenses are down; she's relaxed. And neither one of us wants to be anywhere else but here.

"I feel like a kid again," Danni said. "Remember what it was like to dig your toes down into hot sand?"

"You can still do it."

"Yeah?"

"Yeah."

"I wouldn't exactly call this hot," Danni said, burrowing her feet in the sand, "but it still feels good."

"Lots of hot things feel good," Jenny said, smiling at Danni.

"Like what?"

With her index finger, Jenny traced the outline of Danni's lips. "Oh, I can think of lots of things."

Danni looked at her through a drunken haze. "Tell me a few."

Wanting to test the waters, uncertain how far to go, she merely smiled, "Soon."

"Soon?" Danni said. "If I don't eat soon, I'm going to pass out right here on the sand!"

"Let's walk a bit before we go in," Jenny said, "I think we both need the fresh air."

As they stood, Danni threw an arm across Jenny's shoulder, then it dropped back to her side. The two women walked along the water's edge hand in hand. As they walked, neither spoke. "I'm starting to sober up real fast," Danni finally said. She dropped Jenny's hand and gestured in the direction of the restaurant. "Let's go — it's still early enough to get a table by the water."

IX

Danni spent more time than usual thinking about her party. This year, she decided, she would hold it at the yacht club. As always, it would be a formal affair for clients, business associates, family, friends and neighbors. Though she might be a source of scandal to many of these neighbors, not one of them would think of declining her invitation. Her Labor Day parties had become something of a tradition in Baysville.

When she suggested that Jenny plan the menu, she was surprised at how enthusiastically her friend entered into the spirit of it all. She overheard more than one phone conversation of Jenny's with the caterer, and although the complete menu hadn't been decided upon, Danni knew that this would be a very special event.

In the easy sharing of responsibilities which had evolved between the two women, it did not seem unusual for Jenny to take charge of the menu, and her party. Jenny's energies and enthusiasm seemed to be boundless.

Danni had begun to see her own home through Jenny's eyes. She now realized how much attention was actually required to keep the large house in running order. Jenny had taken charge of a multitude of household projects that included everything from having the chimney cleaned to repairing the dishwasher. Even small jobs were taken care of: a cellar window lock replaced, a leak in the roof patched, shrubs long overgrown trimmed and shaped, window boxes built for the windows at the back of the house.

Wanting to do something special to thank her, Danni told Jenny she'd like to pick out the gown she'd wear to the party.

Jenny accepted, but told her, "Don't go to any special trouble. I can promise you there's not another occasion where I can see myself wearing anything other than what I have on."

"If you can get through life in shorts and a T-shirt, fine. But you never know — I might introduce you to Prince Charming."

"I'd be very surprised if you did," Jenny said.

It had taken only one visit to Botticelli's for Danni to select her own gown, a black crepe with plunging neckline and back. But she couldn't decide what Jenny should wear. Odd that Jenny had so little interest in clothes, especially after her years as a model. She seems to have put all that behind her, Danni concluded as she walked through the Public Garden on her way to Copley Square.

Brilliant red geraniums and pale pink and white begonias bloomed in well-tended flower beds. Danni paused under the graceful weeping willows surrounding the pond now traveled by swan boats carrying laughing children, smiling adults.

Boston's Back Bay was bright and exciting that afternoon. Sidewalk cafés bustled with activity as students, young matrons, and businessmen and women walked past elegant Newbury Street shops. Street musicians were playing Mozart, violins carrying the melody over the sound of traffic. A short distance away the John Hancock Building presided over all, images from the Copley Square Trinity Church and even the clouds themselves reflected in its stately glass tower. Danni looked up and smiled as the sun shone down out of the blue summer sky.

Exhilarated, Danni was surprised when she walked into Serena's and found herself the only customer. All the better, she thought, her attention caught by a flow of color at the back of the room. Seconds later she held the dress in her hands — a deep green crepe de chine, the fabric making the color almost luminous, as if she were looking into pools of the night. Thin straps connected the bodice to the back; the waist was tightly fitted and a slit ran up the left side of the dress. Perfect for Jenny's long legs. How could any dress look more beautiful on her?

Danni left the shop even happier than when she'd found her own dress. Why was this so exciting, she asked herself. But her mood wasn't the kind to promote answers.

After purchasing the gown, choosing a date for Jenny was easy. Danni knew more than her share of attractive men, and she soon settled on Stan Mitchell, an assistant D.A. He made a point of being seen with only the loveliest women in Boston. Jenny surely qualified there, Danni thought.

X

Three days before the party, the rains began. Danni had lived through hurricanes that had swept the eastern coast, and although it was too early in the season for such a storm to hit, this weather had all the feel of one. There had been a sudden drop in temperature the night before as winds tossed clouds across the sky, creating an eerie view of the stars and moon until cloud cover blanketed the heavens.

On her way home, the torrential storm forced Danni to pull off the road. Two cigarettes later — impatient with sitting in the steamy car — she decided to make the best of it and drive on.

The streets of Baysville were deserted; the harbor was shrouded in mist; the steeple of the white Congregational Church was barely visible. Few cars were on the road and though shops were still open in the town square, there was no one about. She made her way down Bay Road, the storm from the east whipping the rain against her car. Once home, she ran to the house; she was soaked through in seconds. Jenny met her, a towel in one hand, a thick terry cloth robe in the other.

Jenny knew that Danni usually had a martini before dinner. While Danni was taking a hot shower, she decided to try her hand at mixing a drink. She slivered the lemon peel, poured the gin, waved the vermouth bottle letting a drop, perhaps two, escape, and stirred the mixture with a thin glass rod. Danni stepped back into the kitchen wearing the white robe.

"You must have read my mind," she said, seeing the martini.

"I hope it's dry enough," Jenny said.

"Perfecto," Danni replied, savoring the taste of the chilled gin. "I'm a new woman."

They enjoyed a leisurely dinner, the kind of meal that signaled a break in the routine of scheduled lives that sometimes only a storm can bring. Danni had decided that she really didn't have to do any paperwork that evening, and she certainly wasn't going out, so why not play a game of hearts with Sara?

As they began their fifth game, Jenny mentioned that *Dark Victory* was on the 9 o'clock movie.

Danni said, "I haven't seen that in years. Why don't we watch it?"

The game soon over, Sara kissed Danni goodnight and walked up to her bedroom holding Jenny's hand.

"Strange night," Danni said as Jenny returned to the living room. "Have you noticed the glow in the sky?"

"Beautiful, isn't it? The moon's nearly full, and the wind must be thinning out the clouds. The worst of the storm is over."

"I hope so."

Danni motioned for Jenny to join her on the couch. When she threw the back pillow onto the floor, the couch seemed nearly as wide as a twin bed. "Come on, there's plenty of room to stretch out," Danni said. "Let's be comfy."

Sitting next to Danni, Jenny knew what she was feeling just having their legs touch. How could she lie down beside her, and how could Danni feel none of this? Yet it was obvious that she didn't, at least not in the way Jenny did, though she had grown more affectionate with Jenny and often reached out to touch her. A few days ago, she'd even given Jenny a warm spontaneous hug when she told her about a new client she'd just signed to a hefty contract. But Danni had moved away from any response to her affection, as if she always had to be in control.

In so many ways, Jenny thought, it's been such a good summer. Why can't I accept it at face value and let it go at that? Why do I have to be in love with her?

Because I am, she thought, I am.

She'd been patient over the past weeks, content just to be with Danni, to share those times of the day with her that had grown to be most important. If she did take the initiative, if she was aggressive with Danni, she might lose her altogether. Yet how long could this go on? Not much longer, not much longer at all, Jenny thought, feeling Danni's hand on her arm.

"Turn the sound up a little will you?" Danni asked.

"Sure." Jenny pressed the remote control.

The movie began. Jenny leaned back on the sofa beside Danni, their thighs touching. Jenny had a hard time concentrating.

"Marvelous shots," Danni said. "And look at that face, those eyes. Ever seen anyone else quite like Bette Davis?"

Even if Jenny hadn't been lost in thoughts of her own,

the question needed no answer. She felt her body flow into Danni's; she felt warm all over, hot.

I'm going to have to break with Anne, she told herself. I can't continue a sexual relationship with her, no matter what happens here. It's not fair to either one of us. When I'm with her, I feel my body yearning for Danni's. When I hold her, I wish she were Danni. Somewhere within herself, Danni must want me; she must.

As if Danni could read her mind, her fingers grazed Jenny's thigh. "Comfy?" she asked. "There's lots of room."

Without answering, Jenny lay down beside her, the length of their bodies touching. Neither woman spoke.

Jenny listened to the dying storm. The wind was from the south, spattering rain against the windows; thin branches of the peach tree tapped against the panes. Where are her feelings tonight, Jenny asked herself. Why don't I take the chance and —

"Isn't this one for the books," Danni interrupted her thought. "Two broads like us home watching TV. We should be out breaking hearts, Jenny, or at least having a good time. What do you say one of these nights when you're not off with Romeo, we go out on the town?"

Jenny sat up. She was annoyed, whether at herself or Danni she wasn't sure.

"Of course, you'd be competition for me," Danni said. "I don't know if I could take it." Playfully she slapped Jenny's leg.

"We're probably attracted to different types — redheads, that's my weakness," Danni said.

"So that's why you were so taken with Sara and me —"

"I was, for sure, but right now I'm talking about red-headed men."

"I've always been partial to blondes myself," Jenny said. She decided to say no more. They both fell silent.

The drone from the TV woke Jenny sometime in the

middle of the night. She turned off the set. The rains had stopped; in the sky to the north she could see the moon again.

She got up and opened the closet for an afghan, thinking she would cover Danni and then go to bed, but she turned out the light and spread the throw over them both.

Aware of the closeness of Danni's body, she resisted touching her. But Danni turned in her sleep and wrapped an arm around her. Jenny moved toward the sleeping beauty, brushed the fine blonde hair back from her eyes, and gently kissed her forehead.

Moments — perhaps hours — later, Jenny was awakened by Danni's body moving against her own. Her legs were twined in Jenny's and she rocked back and forth in a rhythm Jenny began willingly to respond to until she realized Danni was in a deep sleep. Where is she, Jenny wondered; what dream has her now? Her hands glided the length of Danni's body, gently caressed the small of her back. Slowly, insistently, the rhythm continued; Danni's arms held Jenny tight. Night was a blanket of comfort for Danni and she rocked in its warmth. Back and forth she moved, slowly back and forth. She sighed as sleep held her peacefully in its embrace. Lulled by Danni's movements, Jenny felt herself gliding into her own world of dreams.

Then Danni pulled away from Jenny. Startled, she struggled to sit up. "Where am I?" she asked, her voice like a lost child crying in the night.

"Sssssh," Jenny said, "come back to sleep. You were dreaming, just dreaming."

"Dreaming," Danni said sleepily, "how do you know?" Comforted by the closeness of Jenny's body, Danni knew she had to move away. Why is that such a hard thing to do, she asked herself. Then Jenny's arms enfolded her and Danni lay her head on her shoulder, telling herself that soon, very soon, she would move.

XI

By the morning of the party, Jenny had won the heart of the temperamental catering chef. Having cooked in Vienna and Paris before arriving in Boston, he had set ideas on what would be not only appropriate, but appreciated; and he was accustomed to presenting a menu to a client who was pleased with it, sometimes even overwhelmed.

This young woman wanted the hors d'oeuvres and buffet served her own way — explaining that the key word for the menu was a phrase written over a hundred years ago by a New England philosopher — simplify, simplify. Thinking of the final astronomical sum of the bill, he smiled. Sometimes it was much more costly to simplify. Still, he had to agree it was all in good taste.

Instead of his usual delectable hors d'oeuvres, she wanted

an oyster bar. What could be simpler? For those not inclined toward oysters, there would be pea pods stuffed with capers and fresh cream cheese, a bluefish pâté and Gulf shrimp. The buffet would offer a choice of chilled lobster, poached salmon or rare roast beef with an accompanying salad niçoise.

He remembered asking her: This is a simple meal? And her answer: Of course.

Ah, why fight such a lovely woman, he thought; we all have something to learn in this life.

* * * * *

Danni had made a late afternoon appointment with her hair stylist on Friday, the day of her party. She and Garth would meet at his apartment in the city, have a drink together and leave from there. Though she and Jenny had spoken by phone several times, they wouldn't be seeing each other until that evening.

She was intrigued by the notion of Jenny in the emerald green gown — and curious to see the expression on Jenny's face when Jenny saw her own plunging black dress. One thing's sure, Danni thought, they'd be the two best looking women there.

* * * * *

Beth Drew and Stephen had driven to Connecticut for the long weekend. Ethel had suggested that a very reliable young woman from Hope House would no doubt be happy to spend the day and evening with Sara. With Sara happily occupied, Jenny had the rest of the day to devote to the party and herself.

Though Jenny was looking forward to Danni's party,

she had wearied of the summer charade. It could not continue through the fall. She could no longer separate the deep feelings she had for Danni from the job she'd grown to enjoy. She would have to leave. Where would she go this time?

Whatever move she made, it wouldn't be toward Anne nor back to New York. She belonged here now — if not in this house, somewhere in this town. She'd find other work, finish school, begin a different kind of life for herself and Sara, a life not so dependent on others, on any woman . . .

All I want tonight, she thought, is a sign. Some sign, some move so that I know Danni's aware of what I feel for her.

She knew that one way to get Danni's attention was to dazzle her, and dazzle her she would — and could.

Jenny knew how to use makeup in a way that few women did. She knew the secret that all great models shared: that by a subtle change of hairdo or makeup, a face took on a completely different appearance.

* * * * *

All her life Jenny had been told she was beautiful. "What an exquisite child," was a phrase she'd heard often during early childhood. When she lingered in front of the mirror, her mother had applauded her vanity.

Jenny had loved touching her long red hair, winding it around her fingers, brushing it over her shoulders. In the mirror she explored the depths of her eyes, ran her small hand over her lips, traced her features in the way many grownups had. She lived a charmed life as a child: loved, pampered and adored; she had learned how to get what she wanted. But as she grew older she also learned that beauty brought her as many enemies as friends. Gradually she found a place for her real self behind her beautiful facade and with time, became indifferent to her beauty. Let others yearn for it; she did not care.

As a young woman, her beauty and coolness became most attractive to men.

Peter was a fashion photographer. There was no doubt that he loved her, but he did not have the insatiable desire, as other men did, to own her, to possess her completely. Theirs was a typical enough courtship and marriage as far as their world of fashion was concerned, and Jenny fell in with Peter's crowd quickly, liking the people he spent time with, liking the fact that he gave her enough space to get to know other people.

Once they became lovers, the thought of infidelity never occurred to her. Why would she want anyone else when she had him? When she became pregnant with Sara, they married, their wedding informal and great fun — like a spur of the moment party, one of their friends later said.

Their friends saw them as the perfect couple, fun to be with, and obviously in love with each other. Because they did love each other, Jenny was shocked and incredulous when another model claimed that Peter and Heather Farnsworth, the agency's other top model, were still lovers.

"Is it true?" she asked him.

"You really want the truth?" he answered.

Sara was less than a year old when Jenny left Peter. They continued to see each other occasionally. Peter came for Sara every Saturday morning, and from time to time Jenny and Peter were on the same assignment, but as the months passed, they had less and less to say to each other. Eventually, Peter's interest in his daughter waned; his contact with her became limited to holidays.

Following the separation and divorce, Jenny had had lovers, but she was weary of these men who worshipped her, who put her on a pedestal of their own imagining. She found herself admiring two of her modeling friends who were lesbian lovers; they had made no secret of their preference for each other. Although she had yet to explore the motivation of their attraction, perhaps it was that like was drawn to like, beauty to beauty. Even this made more sense than her own sterile relationships.

Jenny had been on location in New Mexico when she first met Margo Cannon, a model who had been flown in from San Francisco for the assignment, just as Jenny had been flown in from New York. The Lunar Cosmetics project, targeted for the September *Vogue,* was extensive enough that Jenny had to arrange for two weeks of child care for Sara, who remained in New York.

A model friend of hers had mentioned that Margo Cannon was gay. As the days passed in New Mexico, Jenny looked at the beautiful black model with increasing interest and curiosity. They began to spend time together.

One evening, after another day of long hours spent in uncomfortable poses, Margo suggested they have dinner together in her room.

"Something light," she said. "We can unwind over a salad and iced tea, all right?"

Jenny agreed, pleased by Margo's suggestion. She was intrigued by this woman. And, she admitted, curious about Margo's reaction to her.

After a shower, Jenny pulled on a pair of levis and a red T-shirt, and walked down the hall to Margo's room. She was nervous; she knew she was responding to a sense of mystery about all that Margo represented. On the set that day, she had felt excited in Margo's presence and knew that the feeling was mutual.

Margo answered the door wearing a purple satin robe tied loosely around her waist. Her dark skin glistened; she ran a hand through her short afro.

"Do you mind if I don't dress for dinner?" she asked.

"Hardly," Jenny laughed. "I'm not exactly formal my-self."

"So relax — make yourself at home — we've worked hard today. Can I get you anything? Ice water? Coke? Grass? I never like to travel alone. How would you like me to do your I Ching?"

"You're offering a hell of a lot all at once," Jenny said lightly.

"I haven't even told you what I really want to offer you."

Margo walked over to Jenny and, ever so gently, traced her face with the tips of her fingers. "I've wanted you all day," she said. She took Jenny's hand and led it to the purple sash of her robe. "We'll be beautiful in bed together."

Jenny wound the ends of the sash around her fingers. "I'm not sure," Jenny said tentatively, "I don't know . . ."

"You don't?" Margo smiled. "Then trust me. You want to, don't you?"

"Yes," Jenny whispered. "It's just that I've never —"

"Don't be scared, baby." Margo's voice was soft, seduc-tive. "We're here all by ourselves . . . just you and me . . ."

Still unsure, Jenny closed her eyes, unwound the sash and caressed the satin, the fabric cool and smooth and silky. Margo's lips brushed her own in the lightest of kisses; Jenny's breath quickened with desire; her fears dissolved. She untied the sash and let it fall to the floor.

Margo's hands were on Jenny's waist. She lifted the shirt, pulled it over Jenny's head, dropped it onto the floor and slowly caressed her breasts. Jenny felt her own hands move to Margo's body, touching warm, firm breasts, exploring taut nipples tentatively, wonderingly. Then she watched while Margo slipped the levis down and off her, running her hands up the inside of Jenny's legs, savoring Jenny's wetness, her want. Excited, Jenny clung to her, embracing her shoulders, her back, her soft, sweet skin.

The next morning, back in her own room Jenny could think of nothing but the hours she'd spent with Margo, marveling at the intensity and passion in their lovemaking.

When she had walked to Margo's room, she had anticipated that something would happen — a mild flirtation at least, perhaps more. What she hadn't expected was Margo's directness and her own sudden explosion of response. Excitement, desire, passion — she'd felt all of these with greater intensity than she had ever known. And the sweet tenderness of making love with a woman . . .

She longed to be with Margo again. All that busy day on the set, she thought of nothing but the pleasures of the night to come.

As she was leaving for the day, Margo found her, put her arms around Jenny's waist, kissed her on the cheek.

"Love to see you tonight, darling, but my agent's just flown in from the coast. Tells me he's got *big* business brewing. Let's get together real soon, though."

They were never alone again. Had it been only five years ago, five years between that moment and this?

Five years of drastic change, Jenny reflected. Divorced, living on her own with Sara, she had begun to explore the world around her. She found herself turning to women more and more; nothing seemed as natural to her as a woman's body, as comforting and beautiful.

Other values in her life were changing as well, changes that had begun when she gave birth to Sara. As agencies looked for younger, fresher models, choice assignments were at a premium for her. She had grown tired of the frantic pace, weary of the competitive edge. . . . And she had begun to question her profession, its treatment and attitude toward women.

She thought of the years ahead and all that was possible for herself and Sara. She wanted a safer environment for her child, a quiet life; she wanted to leave the city. In the year after her divorce, she took courses at the New School and focused her energies on a craft she'd first learned in college, rediscovering the pleasures of weaving. She explored the world around her with the many women she met and began attending concerts and lectures, visiting bookstores. With the encouragement of her new friends, she moved easily into the women's community.

And then, Anne Yarwood had entered her life. Strong and assured, successful in her own career, Anne offered Jenny the encouragement she needed when she spoke of going back to college to complete her degree. Anne promised her that Boston or the nearby coastal communities would offer the quality of life Jenny wanted for Sara and herself. In the end, though Anne's support was essential, the decision to move to New England was one Jenny made independent of her feelings for Anne.

Once accepted at the university and settled in Baysville, Jenny became aware that in contrast to her professional self, Anne was cautious and tentative in her personal life. She offered Jenny no more than what they presently had: an affair.

Yet it wasn't all that easy to break things off. She hadn't made many friends. Until Danni. She hadn't really felt at home here. Until Danni. And she knew that she hadn't been in love before. Until Danni.

Danni was the woman she had longed for, had dreamed of. Jenny looked at herself in the mirror and said silently, Love me, Danni. Want me.

She would use every trick of her former trade. She would make herself so beautiful that Danni could not possibly ignore her.

Tanned from the long afternoons of sailing in the sun, her body glowed. Her softly curling auburn hair shone. Expertly, she emphasized her high cheek bones, accented her green eyes and long eyelashes.

She slipped on the gown Danni had given her. If it had been made for her, it couldn't have fit more perfectly. Jenny admired both the long slit running up the left side of the dress and the reflection of her leg in the mirror. Her shoes were thin straps of silver. She chose a pair of antique silver earrings, a simple silver bracelet. She added a shimmer of silver to her lipstick, then she stepped back and looked at herself in the full-length mirror. She nodded. She was satisfied.

Jenny's date arrived. As she walked down the stairs to meet him, she realized she hadn't given a thought as to what he might be like. Tall and thin, short sandy hair brushed back from his forehead, he looked friendly . . . pleasant.

At the sight of her, Stan Mitchell sighed and thought, I've died and gone to heaven — I have, I surely have. He gurgled hello.

Her self-confidence confirmed, Jenny smiled and extended a hand. Introductions finally made, they walked to the car for the short ride to the yacht club. As they drove into the parking lot, Stan had recovered sufficiently to try some conversation.

"This should be a great party," he said. "If there's one thing Danni knows, it's how to have a good time."

"I hope you enjoy yourself," she said, and Stan suddenly had the strange feeling that he was going to this party alone.

XII

Danni and Garth arrived early at the yacht club, Danni thinking that last minute problems might require her attention.

"Seems like Jenny's managed it all without a hitch," Garth said.

Waiters were bringing out chilled bottles of champagne and tray after tray of hors d'oeuvres. The band was tuning up. Sprinklers freshened the lush green lawns, several miniature rainbows arching their way through the spray. The dock, already lighted for the evening, led out onto a calm sea and high tide. In the distance the tallest buildings of the Boston skyline were bathed in golden light. The sun was low in the sky, heavy, hot. Sails in the harbor were awash with gold; the sea cerulean blue.

Danni said, "I wonder where Jenny is."

"Relax, she'll be along. We're an hour early."

Garth looked at Danni. In that black gown she was a knockout. He smiled at her, "Let's have a drink."

"All right. We deserve it, don't we?" Danni said humorously. "Even though we haven't done any of the work."

"In my book," he said, "paying the bills *is* doing some of the work. And this is going to cost you a pretty penny."

"My once-a-year extravaganza, Garth. Why shouldn't it be spectacular?"

Garth said, "You're happy these days, aren't you, Danni?"

"Yes, I'm very happy." Though she knew why, she didn't say: Jenny and Sara.

As more and more guests arrived, Danni and Garth moved off into separate circles of conversation. She was laughing and joking with a group from her agency when there was a sudden hush in the hum of party conversation. Danni turned to see Jenny walking toward her.

For Danni, time seemed to stop. Jenny was an exotic creature she'd never seen before.

"Hi," Jenny said.

"Hi."

"Is that all you can say?"

"Well, you're really something," Danni said softly.

"And so are you," Jenny replied, knowing by the expression on Danni's face that she'd made the impact she'd wanted to make.

"I'm speechless — something new for me, I guess."

"Why?" Jenny asked, as she smiled. "You gave me this dress, remember? And it's not exactly what I wear most days, remember?"

Jenny felt a sexual current running between them. She couldn't take her eyes off Danni. Set off by the sharp lines of the black dress, her flesh glowed in the early evening light. And she knew that finally Danni was responding to her as she had dreamed that she would.

"In case you don't know it," Danni said as casually as she could, "you're the most beautiful woman here tonight." Danni quickly ran a finger down Jenny's arm. "If that neckline were any lower . . ."

There was no doubt in Jenny's mind that Danni was flirting with her. "Well," she said, "you could be in a paddy wagon yourself, baby. Your dress — it's stunning. Wouldn't it be kinder to leave something to the imagination?"

"Mother always said you can't go wrong with basic black."

Both women laughed. As a waiter walked by with a tray of champagne, Danni took two glasses and handed one to Jenny.

"Here's to us," Danni said, touching her glass to Jenny's. "I think we're quite a team."

"Yes, we are," Jenny said, her eyes not leaving Danni's as she sipped the champagne.

"And who do we have here?" Garth asked, walking up and putting an arm around Jenny. "I suppose you two are quite aware that you're literally stealing the show."

Stan Mitchell emerged from the crowd. Garth shook his hand. "You're a lucky fellow tonight, Stan."

Stan beamed. "I'd say we're both pretty lucky. Danni, you should have warned me about this beauty. I wasn't prepared. Why've you kept her a secret?"

Danni looked at Jenny and smiled. "Once you give your secrets away, they're gone forever. What do you say we circulate awhile?" Danni strolled toward a small group of friends who were standing nearby.

Garth smiled. "Excuse me, I think I'll follow suit." He moved to Danni's side, then walked across the lawn where old friends had gathered.

Stan hovered over Jenny who continued to be oblivious to his presence. "Are you all right?" he asked.

"Yes," she said, "but I see an old friend. Will you excuse me?"

She walked across the terrace toward Anne Yarwood. What on earth was she doing here?

Anne stepped away from her escort; she was grinning like a Cheshire cat. "Surprised to see me?" She embraced Jenny.

"Of course I am," Jenny said, turning her cheek to Anne's kiss.

"Harry Willis invited me, and after all you've been telling me about this party, I just knew I had to keep an eye on my baby." Anne was staring at Jenny. "Where *did* you get that gown?"

"A small Newbury Street shop, Serena's. Do you know it?"

"I didn't realize you were making the rounds of the fashion salons. You should call me for lunch when you're in the city. I can always take an extra hour off here and there."

"You look very nice yourself, Anne," Jenny said, looking over her simple white gown.

"Too tailored for your taste, I'm sure. But at least I didn't wear a tux."

"Maybe you should have," Jenny said, smiling. "Think of all the stir you'd cause."

"Tonight it's just you and Madame Danielle causing the stir."

Jenny looked at her.

"I can see where you are with her," Anne continued evenly. "You're not fooling anyone. But you're wasting your time. She wouldn't touch you with a ten-foot pole."

"I don't know what you're talking about," Jenny evaded, not wanting a confrontation with her now.

"Oh sure. You haven't taken your eyes off her. I know

you too well. It might not be obvious to a crowd as straight as this one, but it sure as hell is obvious to me."

Jenny saw Danni standing at the edge of the lawn talking to one of the waiters. She moved away from Anne, wanting to escape. "There seems to be a problem with one of the waiters."

"Problem?" Anne said, "I don't think so. I think you —"

Jenny said impatiently, "Stop acting like a child. I work for her, you know." And she walked off, toward Danni and the handsome young man she was talking with.

"Hi," Jenny said. "Need any help?"

Danni turned to her. "No, Tony's an old friend. Or maybe a new friend. Whatever. We were just having a private conversation. He'd like to go sailing with us sometime."

"Sure would," Tony said, obviously relishing Danni's attentions.

"So we'll talk later," Danni said to Tony. "Time for you to get back to work now and me to get back to my party."

Jenny felt disappointed by Danni; she wanted everything about tonight to be special; she didn't want Danni involved with anyone but herself.

"Just another young stud," Danni said with a shrug. "The world's full of them."

There was a heady excitement in her voice that Jenny had never heard before. "Everything going all right?" Jenny asked. "With the party?"

"You can see for yourself — it's a great success. All your doing. I know how much time and effort you put into it."

"I enjoyed every moment. It's been nothing but pleasure."

"Well, it's certainly taking care of itself right now. Let's take a break, get away for a minute. It'll be a long evening from the look of things."

As they talked, Danni and Jenny strolled down the lawn toward the water. A path of purple light led them to the dock; they moved further and further away from the party.

"From here you'd hardly know what's going on up there," Danni said, reaching for Jenny's hand.

The sun had set; they stood in the shadows listening to waves slap against boats moored close to the dock.

"How can I thank you for all the help you've been?"

"Oh, I can think of a few ways," Jenny said, her fingers quickly dancing down Danni's arms.

"I'll bet you can," Danni answered in a whisper.

The sensuousness of Jenny's caress thrilled Danni in a way she'd never known before. She was intrigued by the seductiveness of Jenny's tone, fascinated that she was responding to her as she was. Strange as these feelings were, they were exciting. She was discovering a new side of Jenny — and of herself. She wanted the feelings to continue, but she was overwhelmed by what was happening. She needed to calm herself, to ease the situation.

"You're sweet, Jenny, do you know that?"

She intended to move away, but then she lightly kissed the tip of Jenny's nose, her forehead, her eyes. . . . She stepped back, leaned against the railing of the dock. Their fingers now entwined, Danni found she could not break away. She felt confused, unsure of what was occurring. "Well, as I said, thanks," she said softly.

As if from afar, she watched herself turning back to Jenny. Gently, she caressed Jenny's face, her neck, her shoulders. Then her hands rested lightly at Jenny's waist. She could feel her body through the smooth, satiny material. "Do you think we should go back?" she whispered.

"Not now," Jenny said. "Not yet."

"I wanted — just wanted to thank you . . ."

"You have . . ."

It seemed the most natural thing in the world to be holding Jenny in her arms. Her hands moved across Jenny's back, the skin warm, soft, as smooth as the fabric of her gown. Her fingers roamed through Jenny's thick hair, exploring her neck, her ears, her beautiful face.

And then they kissed. Slowly, Danni enjoyed the sweetness of her lips. She tasted the tip of her tongue, ever so lightly. Then her mouth savored Jenny's, lingeringly, passionately. She was shaken by her own excitement.

Jenny returned her caresses, her embrace, holding Danni in her arms, adoring her with her kisses. As their lips met yet one more time, Jenny wanted their kiss to last a lifetime. She sighed, passionately; she pressed her body into Danni's. . . . She held Danni's face in her hands, the depth of her kiss rising from the very wellsprings of her soul.

And with Jenny's passion surrounding her, enclosing her, Danni pulled away.

"This is a little more than we bargained for, don't you think?" Danni said, her voice breaking with emotion.

Her words a gentle plea, Jenny said, "I think we should talk about what's happening." She didn't want to lose this.

"What the hell have we been drinking?" Danni asked, hearing voices in the summer evening, laughter from the party. What was happening? How had this gone so out of control? "If anyone saw us — they'd put us in the same boat as Anne Yarwood. She's the town dyke, in case you didn't know."

"I do know."

"Just thought I'd warn you. I saw the two of you talking a while ago. You're just the type she'd like to scoop up." Still sorting through her own emotions, her continuing arousal, she moved away from Jenny.

"Danni, don't run away now. Don't pretend nothing's happened."

"I think we just got a little carried away, that's all," Danni said hurriedly. "I mean, fun's fun, but there's a limit. I'm sure you feel the same way. Let's go back."

She walked down the dock. Jenny, disheartened by

Danni for the second time that evening, followed, then caught up to her. As they returned to the party, the tone of their conversation changed. They spoke almost formally, of the party's success, of the next sailing trip, the end of the season itself — everything except what had passed between them.

Danni looked around for Garth. Jenny, she saw, had continued on to the opposite side of the lawn, and was with a small group from Cabot Advertising.

Agitated, Danni reached for a glass of champagne, aware that her hand was trembling. How could she let something like that happen? What was she thinking of?

I wanted to thank her for all she's done — for all she means — I wanted to — I wanted — Danni couldn't complete her thought.

Across the lawn, Jenny was surprised as Hal Roberts and Marie Harbeck stepped to her side. She hadn't seen either since New York.

"What brings you all the way out here?" Jenny asked.

"Oh," Marie said, "we're both in Boston now — at Cabot Advertising. How about you? How do you know Danni Marlowe?"

"I just happen to work for her," Jenny said, her eyes focused worriedly on Danni.

"I thought you'd gotten out of the trade, my dear," Hal said, waving his champagne glass. "Thought it was all too crass and vulgar for your aesthetic sensibilities."

"I can see you haven't changed, Hal," Jenny said, distracted by his catty chatter. "But I have. If you want the truth plain and simple, I'm Danni's housekeeper."

"Come now, darling, don't bother to play games with me. That's the gorgeous creature over there isn't it? Prowling her turf, is she?"

Jenny prevented herself from jumping in to defend Danni, not knowing what to defend her from — besides, she

knew that whatever she said would only provide fuel for
Hal's running commentary. Hal was right about one thing,
though: Danni was gorgeous. The black gown clung to a
lithe body tanned by a summer in the sun. Jenny thought
of their embrace, the touch of her lips, the softness of her
skin. She was aware that she was smiling and nodding as the
conversation continued, but her mind and her dreams were
elsewhere.

Across the lawn, Danni listened as Lisa Matthews talked
to her about Hal Roberts. "Deadly quiet scene, if you ask
me," Lisa said. "Hal's settled down with Brian and, except
for the beach boys they entice up to Marblehead for oc-
casional weekends, they're very domestic."

Aware that Jenny was looking at her, Danni concentrated
on Lisa's conversation. But then their eyes met and Danni
felt Jenny's touch as fresh in her memory as if it were still
happening, as if they still stood together on the dock in
embrace, their lips touching.

She looked away from Jenny, knowing that if any man
had aroused this much excitement in her she would be out
the door with him in a minute.

What am I thinking? I've had too much to drink. We
spend too much time together, that's all it is. After all,
Jenny has the lover she sees twice a week and what am I
doing? For all the sex I've had this summer, I might as well
be in a convent. And half the time I even take care of Sara
while she goes off for the night with Romeo. Every night
without fail I come trotting home like a good little puppy.

And then she realized for the first time exactly why she
was coming home. There was someone waiting for her. Not
just someone. Jenny.

"Oh my God," she murmured.

"Everything all right?" Lisa asked.

"Yes," Danni said, "I'm fine. Look, I'll catch up with
you later. I think it's time for me to get back into my own

mainstream. And maybe tonight's the best time to start."

When Lisa Matthews walked over to say that Danni, four bottles of champagne in her arms, had just taken off for parts unknown with a very cute, very young and dewy-eyed waiter, Jenny felt sick to her stomach.

"His parts are not unknown to me," Hal said, smirking.

Jenny looked at them both, smiled vacantly, and walked in the direction of the only friend she had there.

Garth nodded, solemnly confirming that he was aware of Danni's absence. "This is going to be hard for you to believe, but I've grown used to these escapades."

"But why? She's talked about this party for weeks! Why would she leave like this?"

"Lots of reasons, Jenny. If nothing else, some of the town people will weave enough scandal out of this to last the winter. Twenty minutes ago there were two stars of this particular show — now there's only one. Maybe she took off to upstage you."

"No, Garth," she said quietly, "I won't buy it — and you don't believe that either."

"All right. Let's just say that Danni was in one of her moods. Look, tomorrow's another day, right?"

Jenny didn't answer. How could Danni do this? Furious with Danni, she was angry at herself as well. Her scheme — and that's what it was — had backfired. After all her plans, after all that had happened between them — not just down at the pier, she realized, but all summer — she'd gone off with a waiter. He was Danni's choice, not Jenny.

It would serve Danni right, she fumed, if I brought Stan Mitchell home tonight. Danni had arranged this blind date; it would serve her right to find us in bed together.

Jenny looked up to see Ethel Marlowe walking toward her.

"Jenny," she asked, "where's Danni? I saw her just a while ago and now she's nowhere to be found."

"She's gone, Ethel. She left the party —"

"She can't leave her own party," Ethel said impatiently. "Was she ill?"

"No, no she wasn't." Jenny's tone was unusually sharp.

Ethel looked at her with concern. "You're upset, dear. What happened? Did you and Danni have words?"

"No. She seemed so excited about the evening — she never seemed happier. We — We —" She couldn't complete the sentence.

"Come to think of it, when I saw her — oh, less than a half hour ago, she seemed distracted." As Ethel looked at the expression on Jenny's face, she realized that some misunderstanding had occurred between the two women. Now what had her daughter done?

A few minutes later, Jenny asked Stan Mitchell to take her home.

Saying goodnight at the door, he asked to see her again. She had no intention of seeing him. Suggesting he call was the easiest way to handle it. She closed the door behind her and walked upstairs to her room.

XIII

Early the next morning, Sara tiptoed over to Jenny's bed. "Time to get up, Mommy?" she asked.

Jenny, already awake, looked at her daughter and nodded.

"Are we going sailing today?"

"I don't know," Jenny said. "We'll see."

"Is it time to wake up Danni?"

"Not yet. Let's squeeze some oranges and make some coffee."

Jenny pushed back the sheet and sat up, wondering if Danni had come home last night. If so, she had been very quiet. As she reached for a pair of shorts and a T-shirt, Jenny glanced out the window; she saw the silver Porsche in the driveway.

During breakfast, Jenny explained to Sara that they were going to let Danni sleep as long as she liked. "You go out and play — I'll call when it's time to come in. And no questions about sailing, okay? I don't think we'll be going out today."

Moments later, as she stacked dishes in the dishwasher, she knew Danni was in the kitchen.

"Any coffee left?" Danni asked, in as close to her normal tone as possible.

Jenny turned and looked at her without answering.

"Guess not," Danni said, turning away. "I'll make some." She dropped a few scoops of coffee beans into the coffee grinder. The hum of the motor was the only sound in the room.

"So," Danni finally said, "enjoy the party?"

Jenny felt her anger swell. "Where in the hell did you go?" she demanded.

Danni reached for a cigarette and took her time lighting it. "It was an easy exit," she said tightly. "I needed one."

"You embarrassed me, you embarrassed your mother, Garth was left to make excuses for you, the people who work for you were smirking, everyone there talked about nothing else the rest of the evening —"

"Don't exaggerate," Danni said, irritated at being put on the spot.

"I'm not exaggerating," Jenny said slowly, forcing herself to speak calmly, softly, her words measured and intense, her anger bringing her close to tears. "Just answer. Where did you go?"

"I needed some air," she said angrily, not wanting to have to explain herself to Jenny, yet knowing that an explanation was the least she owed her.

"And a twenty-one year old waiter has to help you breathe? Who are you kidding?"

"I know you're upset," Danni said, trying to think of

a way to defuse what was happening.

"Oh, I'm upset all right. I'm ready to pack up and walk out of here."

"You're over-reacting. Give me a minute to explain, for God's sake. I didn't sleep with him — if that makes any difference to you. But what if I did?" she asked belligerently. "What is this? The third degree?"

The two women stepped back from each other.

"Isn't there a grain of decency in you?" Jenny asked gratingly. "Are you really so self-absorbed that you don't see what you do to other people?"

"Mother knows me. Garth's a big boy —"

"I'm not just talking about your mother or Garth. Garth must have his own reasons for putting up with you, though for the life of me I can't imagine what they are. But *I* don't have to put up with you. If you want to have sex with children go ahead — don't expect me to condone it."

Danni was caught between two feelings — panic that Jenny would leave and anger for being expected to give her the explanation of feelings she herself could not yet understand.

"I didn't sleep with him," she began, her voice floundering. "What else do you want me to say?"

Jenny's eyes were cold; they offered no comfort. The smile on her lips was cynical. As Danni stepped toward her, she turned away.

Danni could feel her stomach tighten. She couldn't bear Jenny's rejection. "He was just a kid —" As she spoke the words, she knew they were wrong. Angry, she bit off her own sentence. But what did Jenny want from her?

And then she knew — accountability. Something she'd never been able to give another person. She didn't know where to begin — or how — but she knew she had to try.

She looked up just as Jenny threw her cup down, glass

splintering across the floor. "Fuck you," she said in cold
fury and stalked from the room.

* * * * *

Everything's out of control, Danni thought. What the
hell is happening? It's not just that kid she's upset about —
it's what happened between us. Maybe if I tell her that the
party got us too excited — that things like this can happen
between women without their being queer, for Christ's
sake — that it just happened. She's getting herself sick over
it. I've got to tell her: Jenny, I'm not gay and neither are
you. You've got to hear me. I've got to tell you that. We've
got to talk.

But she remembered that she had not been able to forget Jenny the entire time she had been with Tony. She had
had only one vision in her mind: Jenny walking across the
lawn toward her. She could think only of Jenny holding her
close. She could still feel Jenny's lips, her soft gentle touch.

*She can't leave because of last night — because of to-
day — she can't.*

* * * * *

Upstairs, Jenny stood looking out the window. Calm
down, she ordered herself. If you don't, neither one of you
will be speaking to each other.

I need to tell her exactly where I stand. I have to tell
her who I am. How can I expect her to understand unless I
talk to her?

She paced the room, rapidly back and forth. We've got to clear the air; she means too much to me.

She sat down and leaned her head back against her chair. Why did she do it? Why last night? I know she has feelings for me.

Is she denying them? Is that why she ran away? As a smokescreen for what she was feeling? Is she rejecting the whole idea of me? Then how will we ever get through to each other? Jenny closed her eyes and tried to think.

* * * * *

Sara ran into the room. "Mommy, Danni wants us to go sailing. Garth's coming over too."

Jenny looked up and smiled. "I'll bet you're happy about that," she said, her arms open wide for her daughter. It's a beginning, she thought. If we spend the day together, maybe we'll be able to talk. As Jenny smoothed Sara's hair, she realized that after her angry exit from the kitchen, Danni's suggestion of sailing was a peace offering, indeed. She hugged Sara. "Let's go make a picnic lunch."

* * * * *

They sailed a straight course for George's Island. Danni knew that with this wind they would be there in record time. Once anchored, maybe she and Jenny could talk.

The routine tasks required before they could sail out of the harbor and through the channel were performed without much conversation. As they sailed toward the island, spinnakers around them were racing to the east. Like brightly colored balloons, the sails carried the boats across the water. Danni sailed close enough for Sara to see the wide variety of colors and patterns billowing in the wind; stars, stripes, diamonds, hexagons. As each of them picked a favorite sail, the somber mood was broken.

Garth and Sara moved to the front of the boat to fish for flounder, leaving Danni at the tiller with Jenny sitting nearby.

"Sailing was a good idea," Jenny said, knowing that they both felt calmer being on the *Interlude*. "I think it's what we all needed. Sorry I exploded this morning. Things just . . . got out of hand."

In a relieved voice, Danni said, "I wasn't sure there was anything I could do right after this morning."

"Danni, there's plenty you can do right. For now, I just wish you'd explain why you left the way you did last night. Why you really left."

Not wanting to repeat that morning's fiasco, Danni was slow to answer. "I'm not sure — maybe fun and games that weren't very funny." It was the best she could do. She thought for a moment. Fun and games where? Down at the pier, with Jenny? Or out driving along the shore, with Tony? She looked at Jenny to see how she was taking her answer, vague and inadequate as she knew it was. She added casually, "Anyway, I'm here now. In the flesh. Just slightly hung over, but that's nothing new."

Jenny knew she was being deflected, but she thought about the games she herself had been playing. I don't intend any of this as a game anymore, she told herself. I just need the right time to talk to Danni. And it's not here or now, with Garth and Sara close by. She turned to look at Danni. Their eyes met and Danni said softly, "Don't leave."

Jenny wasn't sure she'd heard her. Then she hoped she'd heard her correctly.

"Jenny," Danni said, trying to put some of her churning

thoughts into words, "I don't want you leaving because of what happened down at the pier. I know you're angry at me —"

"Not because of that," Jenny said quickly. "I'm angry you left the party the way you did. I want us to *talk* about last night."

"We will," Danni said, "I promise you. Can we just let it rest for a bit?"

"Okay, Danni," Jenny said, her voice soft and gentle, "we'll give it a little time."

XIV

Reading the latest proposal for a new advertising campaign for Roslyn Designs, Danni was surprised when her
secretary buzzed to announce a call from Jenny. Usually,
she didn't call her at work.

"Any plans for this evening?" Jenny asked.

"No, if all goes well, I'll be out of here by five and home
by six. What's up?"

"Beth Drew's temperature, as a matter of fact. I'd
planned on taking Sara over there this evening — it's Thursday, you know —"

Jenny's night out with her lover. "I know what day of
the week it is," Danni said shortly. "I've got some paper
work to do tonight. Sara can keep me company. Anything
else?"

Taken aback by Danni's brusqueness, Jenny didn't answer for a moment. Then she said, "Plumbing problems. But I'll take care of them."

"What kind of plumbing problems?"

"The drain's backed up in the upstairs bathtub."

"Probably all that red hair of yours going down the drain."

"I don't know." Jenny was perplexed by Danni's hostility. "Maybe. I'll take care of the expense."

"Don't be ridiculous. That's not what I meant. Look," she said, apologizing, "I'm sorry — I'm just having a bad morning. Give Walter Donovan a call, he'll take care of it. And use my bathroom in the meantime."

"Okay. And thanks about tonight. I won't be late."

"You don't have to punch a time clock with me." Danni was aware that her voice had sharpened again. "Hey," she said softening her tone, "I'll see you later. Okay?"

"Sure," Jenny said, "later."

Danni tapped her pen up and down on the desk in agitated rhythm, angry that Jenny was going out. Who was this mystery lover anyway? Why hadn't he ever come to the house? Why hadn't she met him?

Realizing that what she was feeling was jealousy, she threw the pen on the desk. Ever since the pier, she had been acting like a schoolgirl with a crush. She was too old for this. They had to talk, to clear the air.

Then Danni remembered Jenny touching her shoulder that morning, giving her three envelopes to mail, and as Danni reached for the letters, it was all she could do not to take Jenny in her arms again.

"We have got to talk," Danni said aloud, pushing her chair back from the desk. "But talk about what? What am I going to say?"

Damn, she thought. I know Jenny isn't as upset as I am about this — I'm sure of it. It's *my* problem. What am I going to tell her? I owe her an explanation of why I kissed her like that. . . .

"There's nothing I can say," Danni said. "There is no explanation."

She leaned her head back on the headrest of the leather chair. In frustration she closed her eyes and shook her head back and forth. Somehow this would blow over. It would pass. Everything always did. Just let her get her mind off this and get back to work.

She looked at the proposal again; it needed her signature for approval by noon. She reached for her pen and in an automatic gesture signed her name on the cover letter. She left the office.

* * * * *

Jenny laid her robe on Danni's kingsize bed, smoothing the burgundy satin spread before she stepped into the bathroom.

I've been to cocktail parties in rooms smaller than this, Jenny thought as she glanced about. The center of attention was an oversized sunken tub. Sunlight from the overhead skylight filled the room, brightening the stained glass window. Colors from the contemporary orchid design cast a warm glow on the glazed almond ceramic tiles which ran up three walls of the room matching the thick almond rug. A lush Boston fern grew from a brass planter placed at the center of the polished oak Victorian commode. Plum and coral towel sets hung from brass towel racks. Jenny took a face cloth and stepped into the shower stall.

Not wanting any more remarks about red hair in the drain, she reached for Danni's shower cap and slipped it over her head, pushing all the hair inside.

She turned the water on full force. She stood still, luxuriating in the steamy flow cascading down her breasts, over her stomach, down her long legs. Moving the pressure regulator to massage, she turned, relaxing her neck and muscles. God, she thought, this feels good. She rested her arms and head on the opposite wall of the shower and let her body go limp. Steam filled the chamber and life itself seemed sweet.

She knew Danni felt awkward about the encounter at the pier. Danni had asked for time, but Jenny had decided to take a chance. She'd end it with Anne tonight, then tell Danni everything.

Jenny let the pulsating water beat against her breasts and stomach. She rubbed the bar of soap over her body. Aroused by her thoughts of Danni and the sheer luxuriousness of the shower, she lathered her breasts, running circles around the nipples, feeling them harden. Her hand grazed her stomach lightly and moved up and down her legs and thighs, fingers parting the fine hair. She touched herself, wishing it was Danni's hand instead of her own. This only makes it worse, she thought.

Quickly she rinsed her body. For a few seconds she turned the dial to cold, then flipped it off.

Jenny came out of the bathroom as Danni walked into her bedroom. Jenny stood still, not knowing what to do. Then she saw what she had been yearning to see. There was no way that Danni could mask or deny what Jenny now saw on Danni's face, in her eyes.

Danni could feel a throbbing in her throat. She couldn't tear her eyes away from Jenny's body. She wanted to feel that exquisite flesh. She wanted her, all of her. Slowly, she walked over to Jenny. Slowly, she moved her hands down her back, feeling the sensuous line, and rested them on her hips.

Her mouth was dry; her voice was husky. "You haven't dried yourself." Her fingers traced a bead of water down

Jenny's throat.

Jenny's hands clasped Danni's shoulders; her body was trembling and she felt herself holding onto Danni for support, as Danni's finger slowly followed the bead of water. It seemed to pool at Jenny's nipple. Danni's fingers kneaded her breasts, caressed her nipples. Jenny sighed, then reached for Danni's hand, easing it from her breasts to her stomach.

Danni's fingers caressed soft hair, still wet from the shower. Her hand moved easily between Jenny's legs. What her fingers now touched was wet, yes, Danni thought, but so warm. . . .

Jenny breathed into her ear, moaning softly. "Don't stop, not now." The fingers began running circles that had Jenny weak with pleasure.

Once again their lips met, only this time Danni's tongue moved eagerly, feeling Jenny's hot breath in her mouth.

Jenny unbuttoned Danni's blouse and unhooked her bra. She cupped a breast in each hand as Danni wrapped her arms around her.

"Come here," Danni said softly, moving them as one toward the bed.

From underneath the window shrill voices filled the air — Sara and her friends.

"It's mine."

"It's not."

"He took it."

"Oh no I didn't."

Their voices pierced Danni, bringing her to cold consciousness. Abruptly she backed away, furious at what she had allowed to happen. She seized the bathrobe on the bed and flung it at Jenny. "You shouldn't walk around like that. What if the kids came in?"

"They're not going to," Jenny said, tossing the robe onto the floor. "Their squabbles go on like that all day long. We can close the door."

She took Danni into her arms. "You're not getting away from me that easily." She kissed Danni, parting her lips with her tongue. Gently, she caressed her breasts.

She could feel Danni's breath quicken. Then Danni tried to pull back. Jenny wouldn't let go. "What's wrong?"

"I don't know," Danni said, closing her eyes helplessly. "I'm not handling this very well."

"You're handling it just fine."

"No, I — Look," she said, "I'm sorry about the robe — what I said."

She was able to move away from Jenny. Uncomfortable and ill at ease, she stared at the robe, wishing Jenny would put it on.

"That's all right," Jenny said, moving toward her. "Whatever was going on out there has been settled. They'll be calm for at least ten minutes. It's lovely being close to you. Do we have to end it now?" She reached for Danni, held her face in her hands. "You feel wonderful, Danni. Can't we have a few more minutes?"

"You're on your way out, aren't you?"

"I'll call. I'll cancel."

She kissed Danni and covered her lips with quick and tender bites.

"Let me touch you," Danni said, her voice filled with desire.

Jenny led Danni's hand to her body.

"Is this what you want?" she asked, encouraging Danni's caress.

Danni buried her face in Jenny's auburn hair; her fingers were quick and daring explorers.

"Is it?" Jenny whispered. "Is this what you want?"

"I want you," Danni murmured. "All of you."

"Then touch me. I want to feel you —"

"You've got that phone call to make, remember?" The words were a desperate bid for time. "If we go much further we won't be able to stop."

"Is there a problem if we don't?" Jenny asked with gentle insistence.

Danni didn't answer, but she began to move away from Jenny.

"A phone call only takes a minute," Jenny said. "Why don't you answer my question?"

Danni looked away. "Make the call."

Something in Danni's tone warned Jenny not to push further. She picked up the robe.

Danni stood in the living room. The Scotch she'd poured a few minutes ago was gone. She reached for a cigarette; her hands were shaking as she tried to light it. Mechanically, she hooked her bra and buttoned her blouse.

Christ, she thought, I started it. All she did was come out of the bathroom to get the robe.

I've never been into women. I've never had any desire for a woman. But I want her. And I know she wants me. Why push her away? Why try to throw it back in her face? Maybe I need to call Anne Yarwood. She'd have some advice for me.

What a cheap shot. What did she ever do to me except what I tried to do to Jenny? And she didn't get nearly that far.

She was even in love with me — I think. And what did I do when it happened? Acted like I didn't know what was going on. I didn't — then. What an ass I was. I couldn't wait to spread the word through the dorm. How could I have done that to her? And why? I can't think about it now — not with my own situation to unravel.

Ask Jenny to leave? That's ridiculous. One minute I have my hand between her legs and the next minute I'm pushing her away. Go out on the town? That's my usual answer. Got a problem? Drown it in drink. It won't change a thing. If I can just calm down for a few minutes, I can begin to work this out. No matter what, I'm going to see it through. I want her and I don't care what it means. Decisively, she placed her empty glass on the table.

* * * * *

Jenny dialed Anne's number. As she listened to the dull, steady ring, she thought, She can't have left yet. As she was about to hang up, Anne answered the phone, her voice breathless.

"I was just on my way to the car," she said. "What's up?"

"Anne, I hate to beg off at the last minute, but I'm not going to be able to meet you tonight."

"Is something wrong? Should I come over?"

"No . . . nothing's wrong . . . but something's come up —"

"Jenny," Anne said, bewildered by the call, "what is going on? Didn't I talk to you at four this afternoon? Didn't we agree on dinner at The Mooring?"

"Yes . . . I'm sorry to cancel . . . really —"

"Is it Sara? Is she sick?"

"No . . . no . . ." Jenny fumbled for words, for a coherent excuse.

"Then what the hell is happening?" Anne demanded. "You sound strange, Jenny . . . strained."

"I'm sorry. I'll explain it all —"

"What is this? A joke?" As Anne waited for Jenny's response, she remembered Jenny and Danni at the party last weekend. Something was going on out there. If it wasn't with Danni, then who was it? "Jenny, I think you better meet me as planned."

"I can't," she said, in a painful plea.

"Oh, you will, Jenny, or I'll be over to find out why not."

"Anne, maybe we'd just better not see each other . . ."

As Jenny's voice faded, Anne felt sick — then enraged. "You have got to be kidding," she said, her voice rising in anger. "You think a phone call — a half hour before dinner — is the way you're going to end things? What is going *on* out there?"

Jenny did not respond. Her silence was the answer Anne most feared.

"Jenny, you owe me more than this," Anne said softly.

"I know," Jenny said, tearfully, "I'm sorry . . . I'll meet you tomorrow . . . I'll explain —"

"Like hell you'll explain tomorrow. You meet me at The Mooring in one hour or I'll be over there to break that fucking door down."

"Anne, I . . ."

"And we'll see how Madame Danielle likes that."

"Stop . . . I'll see you there," Jenny said, defeated.

Knowing she couldn't risk Anne's anger, Jenny dressed quickly.

"Danni, Danni," she said aloud, "if only I didn't have to leave."

How can I tell her I'm leaving, she thought, tonight of all nights?

As Jenny descended the stairs, Danni walked toward her.

"I have to go out," Jenny said simply, knowing there were no explanations she could offer. "Trust me that I have to do this. I won't be long."

The women looked at each other, their eyes searching each other's face for clues.

Confused, Danni said, "I don't know what's happening. How could you possibly leave now? Who *is* this guy any-way?"

Jenny reached for Danni's hand but Danni backed away.

"I don't want you making love — I don't want you leaving —" Danni's eyes were dark blue; the glints of midnight ice were electric. Jenny moved closer to her. "I'm not going to make love." She asked softly, "How could you even think such a thing?"

Danni seized her. Her hands claimed Jenny's body, her lips met Jenny's in a kiss of angry possession. Her breath was hot; her embrace urgent.

She held Danni, caressing her while she whispered, "You know I want us to be together. It's all I can do to leave you tonight. I have to settle something that should have ended long before this. I need two hours — just two hours — and then I'll come back to you." Her eyes glistened with tears.

Danni's lips lightly brushed Jenny's, and in that whisper of a kiss, Jenny had the answer she wanted.

XV

Once more Danni looked at her watch. Jenny had been gone only twenty minutes, yet she could think of nothing but the moment of her return. She walked into the living room where Sara was stretched out on the floor absorbed by *Sesame Street*.

"Guess what, Sara? We're going out to dinner. Just you and me. Down to The Mooring. You can pick the biggest lobster in the pool."

"I want hamburgers and shortcake," Sara said leaping to her feet.

Danni drove the shore road with swift efficiency. Soon they were escorted into Neptune's Garden, the small room off the main dining area, which was decorated in shades of coral and deep sea green and displayed a collection of rare

Pacific shells. From their table overlooking the harbor, Danni gazed at the setting sun, thinking of Jenny's last words, her sweet caress.

. After dinner, as Sara waited for her shortcake, Danni glanced at her watch again. Then the thought struck: What if Jenny finished her business early, returned early? How could she have been so *stupid* as to leave the house? She would call — if Jenny wasn't there she would leave word on the answering machine that she and Sara would be home soon.

Hurriedly she fished for some change and asked Sara to wait while she made a phone call. Danni saw the waitress on her way to Sara with dessert; she asked her to leave their check on the table.

The phones were located in a small alcove near the entrance and as she dropped in the coins, she looked absently into the bar.

She slammed down the phone. A cold rage sweeping her, she stepped to the table where Jenny sat with Anne Yarwood. She pulled out a chair and sat down.

"What are you doing here?" Jenny asked, staring at Danni in disbelief. "Sara — where's Sara?"

Danni gestured toward the other room. "In there, finishing dessert." She addressed Anne Yarwood. "Legal problems?" she asked sarcastically.

Anne gave her a strange smile. "Not exactly."

She glared at Jenny. "What's this all about?"

Jenny turned away; she could not face the hurt and anger in Danni's expression. She felt numb, stunned.

"Well, it's not too hard to figure out." Jenny's mysterious lover was never a man at all. Furious, Danni turned on Jenny. "I saw you talking with this dyke at the party. I should have known."

"Where the fuck do you get off?" Anne said, her words a curt, angry retort. "So my lover happens to work for the town tramp."

"Your lover," Danni repeated, her voice a hurt whisper.

"Don't look so faint Danielle. You're a big girl. You're not going to fire her just because she happens to be a lesbian, are you? You liberals surely are more broad-minded than that. Or are you?"

"This is all true, isn't it," she said quietly to Jenny.

Anne answered. "Yes, it's true. We're lovers. We've been together for over a year. What's it to you anyway?"

Danni and Jenny looked at each other. Danni felt sick, betrayed and used by Jenny. Tears filled Jenny's eyes; she felt faint.

"Anyone feel like a drink?" Anne asked.

Danni pushed her chair back and stood up.

"Wait." Jenny found her voice. "We have to talk."

"Don't bother. Don't let me interfere with — anything. I want to get Sara home. It's late." She turned her back on Jenny and returned to the dining room.

* * * * *

Anne signaled the waiter for two more daiquiris.

"No, I don't want to stay," Jenny said, staring at Danni's retreating figure.

"Why not? What more is there to tell her?"

That I love her, Jenny answered in her mind, that I'm in love with her, that I have been almost from the moment I first saw her . . . that this summer charade was wrong from the beginning. . . . It's my fault this has happened, but why did she have to find out about Anne and me like this? Will she ever again believe anything I say?

A supercilious smile on her lips, Anne leaned back in her chair and said, "I can't get over the look on her face."

"How could you be so insensitive?" Jenny said angrily. "Did you have to hurt her as deliberately as you did?"

"Hurt *her?* If you only knew —" She broke off, then said, "Have you forgotten the Dear Jane letter you just delivered to *me?*"

"That's *our* issue," Jenny said coldly. "It had nothing to do with her."

"It didn't? Aren't you forgetting why you didn't want to meet me tonight? Why you didn't even want to see me?" There was pain in Anne's voice. "Why didn't you tell her about us? Why didn't you tell her about yourself?"

"I didn't tell her I was gay because I didn't know how she'd handle it. After tonight I wish I'd told her right from the beginning."

"My heart bleeds for the two of you."

Jenny returned to the issue at hand, wanting this over. "I meant what I said, Anne. If we can be friends, all right. Other than that, it's over."

"Give us a chance, baby," Anne said quietly.

"Don't you think anything that was going to happen between us would have by now?" Though she knew she was hurting Anne, she was determined.

Anne took a deep breath. "I don't want to lose you," she said, pleading. "You know I love you."

"Anne, don't —"

"This is my fault. I want you with me, Jenny. Always. We'll start looking for a place . . ." She trailed off, fearing that it was too late to offer what she hadn't been able to give until now.

"That's not it," Jenny replied.

"No? Then what is it?" And then the picture was clear. Furious, Anne said, "It's that slut, isn't it? You want her. Well, I can tell you one thing, if you're wearing your heart on your sleeve for Danielle Marlowe, you might as well paste it back over your tits."

There was nothing else to say. Jenny stood up.

Anne reached out and took her hand. "Think it over, Jenny. We've got a lot of history behind us. We can work things out."

Jenny shook her head. "No, Anne."

Anne said, "I'll come by the house in the next day or so. Now that she knows you're gay —"

Jenny pulled her hand away. "Don't come over. There's no point."

"Maybe to you there's not. I don't give up that easily."

Too proud to follow, Anne watched Jenny walk out of the bar. The waiter brought the new round of drinks and Anne told him to leave them. She sipped the rum and lime juice through crushed ice, finishing one drink, beginning the second. The alcohol dulled her pain without easing her sorrow. Even the shocked expression on Danni's face brought little comfort.

* * * * *

Danni locked her bedroom door, as if to somehow protect herself from the pain she was feeling. Tears filled her eyes; as she tried to blink them away they rolled down her cheeks. Mystery-lover, she thought bitterly. Anne Yarwood, her twice a week fuck. All she's been doing here has been playing me for a fool.

Danni dropped her clothes on the floor and got into bed. She turned out the light and stared into the darkness.

* * * * *

Jenny drove the winding coastal road, trying to gather her thoughts. Returning to the house an hour or so later, she was surprised to see that all the lights had been turned out. The silver Porsche was in the garage; had Danni gone to bed already?

Jenny parked the car, unlocked the kitchen door and flipped on the overhead light. The light seemed harsh, disturbing. She went to Danni's room, hesitated, knocked lightly. Tentatively, she turned the door knob. The door was locked.

In despair, she went back into the kitchen and poured herself a glass of ice water, then looked in on Sara. Her baby was fast asleep. She pulled up the coverlet and bent over to kiss her goodnight. Danni, she knew, would not have said anything upsetting to Sara about the evening's events. She loved Sara as if she were her own child.

In the dark of her bedroom, she looked out into the garden. Bright moonlight cast an aura that held Jenny transfixed. A cool wind blew through the trees. Jenny watched their shadows weave back and forth across the lawn. How could she repair the harm she'd done, the hurt she'd caused?

As she lay in bed, she imagined she heard Danni's footsteps in the hall. Jenny allowed her mind the luxury of fantasy:

Danni opened the door, "I couldn't stay away," she said sitting on the edge of the bed, running her hands over Jenny's body. She pushed back the sheet and lay down beside her. Jenny could smell her hair, her skin, could hear her breathing against her neck. Their bodies were warm as the night. Danni's hands caressed her. Aroused, so aroused, Jenny held Danni close. Then she realized she was holding only her pillow.

Tonight could have meant so much to the two of us . . . And now I can't even comfort her. Of all places, why did I ever ask Anne to meet me at The Mooring?

XVI

Morning brought a cloudy day, the skies seeming on the brink of a downpour. Jenny sat over a cup of coffee and watched Sara play with her food.

After breakfast, with Sara outside in the yard, Jenny stacked their dishes in the dishwasher. Sooner or later, Danni had to come out.

In her room, Danni thought about the day before her. After a sleepless night she had little energy for anything, much less facing Jenny about last night at The Mooring. She felt ill; in the pit of her stomach was a knot she couldn't loosen.

Why would she make such a fool of me? What was the point? And Anne Yarwood, of all people.

Danni looked at herself in the mirror, thinking of how

she and Jenny had touched. Angry at the sudden vision of Anne and Jenny making love, she scattered her jewelry across the dresser.

God damn it, she's not going to know how I feel, that's for sure. Never — I'll never give her the satisfaction.

She ran a comb through her hair, took a jacket from the closet and walked into the kitchen. Ignoring the cup of coffee Jenny offered her, she poured a glass of orange juice.

"Danni, I'm so sorry, I was wrong not to tell you before. I was going to tell you last night. But I had to end it with Anne first. I tried to on the phone but I couldn't. I had to meet her. We have been lovers, yes, but it's over. Don't you realize that?" she asked softly.

"I realize a lot of things this morning that I didn't even think about yesterday," Danni said coldly. "I suddenly have a very clear picture —"

Upset by Danni's tone, Jenny said, "I wish you'd hear what I'm trying to tell you."

"I'm running late. You can save the history of your sexual preferences for later."

Danni put the glass on the counter and walked out the back door.

There was the sound of tires crunching into the gravel driveway as Danni backed into the road and sped off.

* * * * *

Jenny spent the morning trying to put the pieces together. To Danni, this was a betrayal. What had happened in college between Anne and Danni had made everything all the worse.

Thinking about Ethel Marlowe, remembering their conversation, Jenny picked up the phone, knowing Ethel would be understanding.

"You were right," Jenny concluded after telling Ethel what had happened. "I should have been honest with her from the beginning."

"How very unfortunate," Ethel sympathized. "But if the two of you can talk —"

"She's so angry and upset. I have to find a way to talk with her. I think if I had some time alone with her, I could explain myself. Could Sara stay with you a few hours late this afternoon?"

"Of course, Jenny. Why don't you bring Sara over here for the night? We'll have a wonderful time together. She's just what I need to brighten such a gloomy day."

"Thank you so much." Sadly she added, "If only I'd told her before, Ethel. She found out in the worst possible way."

"Blaming yourself isn't the answer. Drive Sara over, then try to relax. You know, I'm very fond of you, Jenny."

* * * * *

Danni told her secretary to cancel her luncheon engagement and to hold all phone calls. She appraised new contracts and planned a trip to New York for the following week, reflecting angrily that she'd spent too many months ignoring important business contacts.

Time to end this little picnic, she ordered herself. Consider yourself lucky. If you hadn't run into the two of them last night, who knows what would have happened?

She tricked me. I took her into my own home, treated her and Sara like family, and all the time not only is she carrying on with Yarwood, but she's planning her seduction of me.

Well, so what if it *had* happened? A single encounter

doesn't mean you're like that. If there's one thing I know about myself after all these years, it's that I'm *not* a lesbian. Nothing happened — and now that I know what she is, it won't.

By 4:00, she'd had all she could take of work. She told June she was leaving and walked from her office to the bar at the Ritz. No point in getting caught in traffic, she told herself.

She sat alone looking out on the men and women walking down Arlington Street. They all seemed to have a destination. At this point, where was she going? She savored the taste of the iced gin, finished her drink, ordered another. It was a quiet evening in the bar. After her third, she decided it was time to drive on home.

The city streets were strangely deserted. Half an hour later, on the shore road, wet leaves flew against her windshield; rain fell in soft pellets around her. She turned into the gravel driveway and parked the car.

XVII

Not wanting to meet Jenny, who was probably in the kitchen, Danni walked toward the front door. It seemed strange entering this way; the house seemed empty. If Jenny's car hadn't been in the driveway, she would have thought no one was home.

She dropped her briefcase on the sofa and went to her room. She stripped off her suit and blouse and thought about taking a quick shower. Restlessly, she looked at her reflection in the mirror. The mauve lace bra and panties were so close in color to her skin that she looked almost nude. As she brushed back her hair, she saw Jenny's reflection in the mirror.

Danni turned to face her. "I didn't think you were here."

"I know. It's quiet without Sara."

Jenny could see pain in Danni's eyes. The kind of day Danni had spent must have been as difficult as her own. The silence in the room grew deeper.

"You're changing your clothes," Jenny said, finally. "I'm sorry to intrude."

"Why?" Danni asked angrily. "Don't you like what you see?" She could feel the explosion within her. All day she'd held it in, swallowed it, kept it at bay. Now, with Jenny only inches away, there was no controlling what she felt.

Jenny looked at her, saw that conversation was hopeless, turned to leave.

"Where do you think you're going?" Danni grabbed her, spun her around.

"I didn't mean to hurt you," Jenny said. "I want you at least to know that."

Danni's face was a blank mask. Jenny reached for her, touched her face.

"Bitch," Danni said, pushing her away. "Now I know. You're Anne Yarwood's whore."

Jenny moved toward her again. "I want to talk to you. You owe me that much. At least listen to what I have to say."

"Listen? Why? I can *see*. You and Yarwood. Of all people."

"Danni, you and Anne have something to settle. I'm not involved in that."

"Is that so? Well, I'd say you're pretty fucking involved in it. I had the sense to say no to her. So — what do you want to tell me? What she's like in bed? What the two of you do twice a week? Tell me what she does to make you come," she said viciously. "Obviously, there's a lot more I still have to learn about life."

"Maybe there is," Jenny said evenly.

"You think so," Danni said. "You think so."

Wanting to ease Danni's anger, Jenny reached out to her.

"You fucking lesbian, get your hands off of me," Danni said with contempt, pushing Jenny away. Then suddenly, furiously, she reached for her, ripping open her shirt with one swift movement of a hand. She seized the waistband of her shorts and tore at it. "Is this what you want? Is it?"

"Don't," Jenny whispered, "Please don't."

"Please don't what?" Danni shouted. "You think I want you? Do you?"

Abruptly, she released Jenny. Jenny stumbled, fought for balance. Danni caught her in her arms. Driven by anger and pain, she covered Jenny's mouth savagely with her own, forcing her tongue into Jenny's mouth.

Jenny struggled to tear herself away from the fierce embrace, sinking her teeth into Danni's lower lip. The skin broke; she could taste Danni's blood.

Danni pushed Jenny away, slapped her across the face. As Jenny stumbled from the force of the blow, as tears welled in Jenny's eyes, Danni felt all her anger dissipate.

Jenny closed her eyes, turned to walk away. Gently, Danni took her arm.

"You're not leaving this room," she said in a whispered command. "You're not going anywhere. I didn't want to hurt you. I've been crazy all day thinking about you and Anne making love."

Jenny saw how she'd hurt Danni, saw how hard it was for Danni to say these words. In her pained expression were vulnerability . . . and desire.

Her hands moved up and down Jenny's body, over her clothing, as if to devour her flesh with her touch. As Jenny's arms clasped her, as Jenny's body pressed into hers, she wanted her out of her clothes. She wanted her naked. Her fingers slid inside the shorts, touching Jenny eagerly.

Jenny pulled Danni to the bed; her cries of passion drove

Danni to move faster, further, deeper. Danni felt a wave of pleasure sweep her body as she continued her thrusts. Then her fingers grew gentle; she touched softly, feeling the tender sweetness beneath her hand. A hot, tingling sensation began to move up Danni's thighs to her groin and this time their tongues met in a hungry searching.

Jenny kissed Danni's eyes, her cheeks, her lips. Danni molded her breasts in both hands; she kissed Jenny's breasts; she sucked her nipples. Her mouth roamed Jenny's body leaving love bites all over her flesh. Sliding the shorts down, she licked Jenny's skin savoring the taste of salt and sweat. She buried her face in Jenny's soft pubic hair, her tongue searching, exploring, then tasting Jenny's full, heady sweetness.

With a rapid staccato motion, she teased her, the tip of her tongue beating a quick rhythm. Then her motions became slower, longer, and Danni's body began to move with hers. Danni loved tasting her, knowing that she was making her swell, knowing she was ready to burst. As Jenny's nails ran up and down Danni's back, Danni concentrated all the more on Jenny's body. It was as if she held a lustrous pearl in her mouth and she treasured it.

"Please," Jenny cried, "please."

Danni could feel Jenny move with the rhythms she created, could feel the spasm that began to shake her body.

"Now," she sobbed, "oh, now."

Her hands in Danni's hair, Jenny held Danni close, her passion growing, mounting, cresting until she pushed Danni away crying, "No more, baby; no more."

Her head pressed against Jenny's wet belly, Danni finally rested. Softly Jenny stroked Danni, winding strands of long blonde hair around her fingers.

Slowly Jenny's fingers traced the lines of Danni's face, caressed her cheeks, her eyes, her lips. She pulled Danni up to lay beside her and held her in her arms. She cradled her like a child and listened to her soft murmurings. Danni's body fell against her like dead weight while she rested.

Jenny thought of how long she had waited for this moment, how long she had waited to hold Danni in her arms. Jenny ran her fingers down Danni's back, traced circles at the base of Danni's spine. Her hand teased Danni, flitting in and out of the silken line that divided her buttocks. She could sense Danni's vitality returning; she knew Danni wanted her to make love. Jenny leaned back and looked at her.

Danni's eyes were still closed; Jenny bent to kiss them, touching the eyelids gently. Then she kissed each of her cheeks, her chin, her nose, her lips. Jenny ran her finger across her bottom lip, touching the blood that had already begun to dry.

"I'm sorry," she murmured, "I'm sorry."

She ran her tongue across Danni's lip and tasted her own essence as well Danni's blood. She kissed her lip and then buried her face in the hollow of Danni's throat. She eased Danni out of her bra and panties, brushed the fabric aside and ran her tongue across Danni's body. Her hands encircled a full breast; her mouth grazed its softness, her tongue and teeth playing with the nipple, now a sweet, hard cone. With her mouth on Danni's breast, she felt she could suck all night. She moved to her other breast and felt the flesh swell and stiffen. Danni's hands touched her shoulders, played with her hair. Jenny could feel Danni's thighs grasping her legs, could feel a motion begin in Danni's body. Jenny lowered her head, her mouth biting Danni gently as she moved from breasts to navel to stomach.

"I want to take my time with you," she said. "I want to go slow."

She looked at the fine, curly blonde hair between Danni's thighs. She blew gently, light wisps of air designed to arouse. She ran her fingers expertly up and down the satiny membrane. Danni was wet and soft and hot. Jenny wanted her, wanted to play with her. She took her clitoris between her thumb and index finger and massaged it as if it were a tiny marble egg.

"Take me," Danni pleaded, her words a low, passionate moan, "take me."

"Give me time," Jenny said, "let me play."

Danni groaned, but her hands on Jenny's head and shoulders assured Jenny she could do as she liked.

Danni felt Jenny's long thin fingers penetrate her with a gentleness she'd never known before, then tease her as part of a playful game. Jenny lowered her face to Danni and kissed the soft skin of her inner thighs, biting her gently before her tongue parted tight curls of golden hair.

"I can't wait much longer," Danni whispered, "I can't hold off."

"Of course you can," Jenny said, exciting her even more with her hands and mouth. "I want to see you. I want to look at you."

She's so beautiful, Jenny thought, as she touched and admired her lover's core. Lightly, she began to trace a pattern of circles with the tip of her tongue. Danni groaned with pleasure as she moved her body to encourage Jenny's love-making.

"Please, baby," she said, "Make me come. Don't tease me. I can't wait, I can't."

Danni's legs began to twitch, and Jenny's arms became a clamp, a vise upon them. Her fingers and her tongue inter-mingled in Danni's body, one hand slipping between her buttocks, the other exploring her vagina as she made passionate love. She could feel the shudders begin to sweep Danni's body as she gave her what she had so long been wanting to give.

Danni felt as if she were drowning. Hot waves swept her body; from her innermost being she could feel herself let go. Short, sweet spasms alternated with delicious waves of pleasure. Danni raised herself, giving herself fully to Jenny's mouth, knowing that all her life she had been waiting to have this moment with a woman. She could feel tears well within her, could taste them as they flowed down her cheeks, over her lips. "Yes, Jenny, yes, yes."

From afar, she heard Jenny say in a hushed whisper, "I want to touch you like this all night."

Danni's body was limp, damp, spent. It was all she could do to reach down for Jenny.

"If you do any more tonight," she said, "I won't be here tomorrow to tell the tale."

Danni's face was still wet with tears. Jenny touched her cheek and lips as Danni kissed her fingertips. Now lying together, their bodies ached, their lips were sore, their skin glistened with the sweat and come of their passion. Danni breathed deeply, taking in the heady scent, bringing Jenny's hands to her lips, tasting herself. Jenny held Danni close to her as she stroked her forehead, her eyelids.

"Happy?" she asked.

"Hmmmmm," Danni answered. "I'm in another world. I feel as if I've been bewitched."

"You have been. The spell's been cast and there's no way to escape it."

As she spoke, Jenny ran her nails over Danni's soft skin teasing her with light scratches. Their legs were intertwined; their toes touched.

"What other magic powers do you have?" Danni teased.

"If I named them, they'd lose their power and they wouldn't be magic. You'll just have to wait and see."

Danni nuzzled Jenny's neck and breasts, blew little kisses over her body. "You're so beautiful," Danni said, "so lovely; my very own weaver of magic."

Danni's touch was a tender caress, but even as Jenny surrendered to it, a cautionary voice warned her that tomorrow would be the dangerous day. She'd had women come out with her before, and the morning after was always a hard one: doubt, regret, anger, resentment, any of these feelings could emerge — as well as passion. With Danni, she didn't know which it would be. She only knew that for tonight, Danni was hers. There were still hours before realization would make its impact on Danni. Why don't I just enjoy them, she thought. Why don't we just enjoy them together?

The women lay together taking in their closeness, listening to the rain. Jenny recalled lines from a poem she had loved since she'd first read it. "Western wind, when wilt thou blow, That the small rain down can rain?" Set to music years ago, the melody played in her mind as she wrote her own words: Now that my love is in my arms . . . we lie in our bed . . .

Jenny leaned over to look at her face. Though her eyes were closed, there was an expression of peace there, and serenity. She'd begun to drift into sleep, and Jenny didn't want to lose her yet. Playfully, she blew in her ear. Danni opened her eyes.

"It's awfully early to go to sleep," Jenny said.

"Who's sleeping? I was just lying here wondering how you feel."

"Oh, pretty nice . . . to put it mildly," Jenny said laughing, as she traced a line up Danni's back with her long auburn hair.

Danni turned and took her in her arms. "I feel as if we're floating in space. Let's not end the night so soon."

"We won't. We have hours and hours before morning just for ourselves."

"What a nice thought." Danni touched Jenny's shoulder, brushed her hair back from her face. "Let me draw a tub for you."

"Sounds wonderful," Jenny said.

While water flowed into the oversized tub, Danni took

out thick towels and a tube of bath oil. Jenny stood in the doorway amused by this unexpected touch of domesticity.

"How do you like your water?" Danni asked. "Hot or scalding?"

"Somewhere in between."

Danni flipped on the switch for the Jacuzzi and the pressure sent waves across the surface of the water.

"Your bath, my dear," Danni said.

She took Jenny's hand and led her. Their bodies submerged in the soothing hot water, both women lay back, sighing with contentment. They were at opposite ends of the tub, stretched out in the churning water, and for what seemed like a wonderfully long time to Jenny, neither spoke as they looked at each other through the steam. Then Jenny sat up, reached for a face cloth, and gently wiped the line of blood on Danni's mouth. The lip was bruised and looked sore; she'd bitten Danni deeply.

"Do you have any salve?" she asked in concern.

"In the medicine cabinet. We'll get it later," Danni said. "I don't need first aid."

Jenny stood up, stepped out of the tub and came back with the salve. She knelt next to Danni in the water and leaned forward. Danni encircled her with her arms and buried her head between her breasts; filling her hands with water, she poured it over Jenny's back. When she took her lips away, Jenny met them with a kiss. Regretting she had hurt Danni, Jenny sat back to apply the salve.

"This will keep the skin soft and moist," she said.

"I can think of other things that would do that."

"We'll have that, too. But let's settle for this right now."

Danni's hands reached below the surface of the water for Jenny's body. She touched her gently, caressed her thighs. "Lie back," Danni said. "Relax."

Jenny let the tube of salve drop to the floor and stretched out again. Her hand moving up the length of

Danni's leg, she lowered herself further into the water to meet her embrace. Jenny sighed with pleasure.

"Water games," Danni said.

"Hmmmm, water games," Jenny repeated.

Playfully, with gentle caresses, they teased and aroused each other.

"I'm having such a good time with you, Jenny," Danni murmured, leaning forward to kiss her.

"Is it always this much fun for you?"

"No. Is it always like *this* for you?"

"No."

"Do you want me to stop?"

"Are you kidding?"

The playful teasing turned to something more serious as Jenny moved closer to Danni. Danni reached for Jenny, pulled her close and kissed her. Their tongues moved slowly back and forth, repeating the patterns they made with their fingers.

Soon Danni tightened her hold on Jenny. "Don't stop," she said.

"Not for the world."

Danni began to move against Jenny's hand.

"Lie still."

"It feels so good. It's never been like this."

Jenny's touch was steady, strong. Danni's body eased even closer; her hands fell across Jenny's shoulders as she kissed her neck, held her tight, and came in her arms.

Danni rested for only a moment. Loving what she knew Jenny was feeling, Danni held her close as Jenny softly moaned. Then both women lay back as circles of water surrounded them.

They held hands, looking into each other's eyes. Jenny knew the dangers of moving too fast, but couldn't help herself. "I'll please you, Danni, more than anyone has."

"You already have," Danni said.

"You liked it with me," Jenny said, wanting to give Danni room to talk about the experience.

"I didn't expect to feel this twice in a lifetime, let alone twice in one night."

"We could have this every night of the week, Danni." Even as Jenny spoke the words, she knew she was expecting too much.

Danni only smiled and said, "You're sweet, Jenny, very sweet." Playfully, she pulled Jenny toward her. "Enough water games for the night. What do you say we get a bottle of wine and go back to bed?"

XVIII

When Danni woke the next morning, sunlight filtering
through the beech tree's leaves cast a pattern of geometrics
on her polished hardwood floors. She watched the pattern
change as wind gently shook the branches. Sunlight seemed
to reach up and touch the edges of the bed. Danni's hand
slowly played with sunbeams, tracing lazy circles through
the light. She felt warm in Jenny's embrace, safe in her
arms and the quiet breathing she heard assured her Jenny
was still asleep.

Danni luxuriated in a feeling she had never experienced.
She had slept well and, without moving too much, she
stretched contentedly. But lovely as all this was, it wasn't
her habit to stay in bed much after she awakened. She was
wide awake and wanted coffee. Lifting Jenny's arm from

her waist, she slid noiselessly out of bed.

She made a pot of coffee and smoked her first cigarette of the day. Sitting cross legged on a stool looking out into the back yard, she drank coffee and examined her body, touching scratches and love-bites that brought back memories of the night before. She tasted her lip; it was sensitive and sore.

Her mind refused to move in the direction of seeking answers for all that had happened. It would take time to absorb it all, time to accept it. For this moment, she was at peace. She experienced a sense of oneness she hadn't known before. She savored the feeling.

She turned toward the door and smiled. Jenny stood before her. She'd slipped on one of Danni's shirts and was rolling up the sleeves as she returned the smile.

"Sleep okay?" she asked.

"Hmmmm," Danni answered, "like a baby. And you?"

"I only woke because I felt you were gone," Jenny said, stepping toward Danni to kiss her.

Danni held her in her arms. "There's a bruise on your face," she said. "I'm sorry."

"It'll fade," Jenny said.

They looked at each other, both knowing this wasn't the time to analyze last night.

"Let me get you coffee," Danni said.

As she turned to the coffee maker, Jenny ran her finger down the length of Danni's back. She leaned toward her and kissed her shoulder. She wrapped her arms around her waist. They stood like that, not speaking, for what seemed a long, long time.

When Jenny finally stepped back, Danni moved toward a chair and brought Jenny with her. Jenny sat on her lap, straddling her thighs, bending forward to kiss her. Danni opened the shirt and then put her arms around her waist. She could smell their sex and was aroused. She could feel

Jenny's breath quicken as her mouth came to Jenny's breasts, as she bit and sucked, first one breast, then the other.

Lightly, Jenny touched Danni's arms. Fully aroused, she guided her hands down the length of Danni's body.

"I want it to be good for you," Danni whispered huskily. "As good as it was for me last night."

"Go slow then," Jenny breathed. "Go slow. Be sweet."

As she felt Danni's fingers slip inside her, she moved against them gently, savoring the sensations that swept her body. Jenny kissed Danni's mouth, her neck. She began a series of swift bites that Danni repeated with the thrusts of her hand.

"Feel good?" Danni asked.

Jenny nodded, breathing yes.

Jenny felt Danni's fingers leave her. She smiled as Danni began to play with her, holding her between her fingers, moving up and down, slowly up and down. She began a circular movement that drove Jenny wild. Jenny's hands fell across Danni's back and she clawed her skin, begging for more. She guided Danni's other hand inside her, led it in a pattern of long, deep thrusts as Jenny sighed and Danni continued her circle of pleasure.

"More," Jenny whispered. "Harder. Fuck me, Danni, fuck me."

Danni stood up. She eased Jenny to the floor, never stopping the rhythm her hand had begun, and lay on her while her own legs straddled Jenny's thighs.

Jenny felt the floor beneath her back, the hotness of her skin, the coolness of the wood.

As if she were drugged, Jenny felt Danni's breasts pressing into her, up and down her body, her lips nipping her skin. She felt Danni's tongue licking her body — her shoulders, her breasts, her stomach, her thighs. All the way down Jenny's body her tongue traced its course until she was sucking her toes, kissing her feet. Then Jenny felt the wetness of her mouth moving up her, biting her ankles, her calves, licking the inner side of her thighs, until Jenny spread her legs and felt Danni's mouth, felt Danni's tongue probe her inner being. Danni took Jenny in her mouth and gave her all the pleasure she knew how to give.

As Jenny's passion grew, she wanted Danni close, wanted her beside her. She reached down and pulled her up. "I want you with me. We're together now. I've never felt like this before. Never. We're one."

She wrapped her arms and legs around Danni and let her passion flow. Danni tried to silence Jenny's cries with her mouth, but Jenny pulled her head away, wanting the sounds to fill the room. Her nails dug into Danni's buttocks: she gripped them tightly, not wanting to lose what was still growing. As Danni felt the spasms begin in Jenny's body, her own movements picked up Jenny's rhythm and she let herself go. Jenny cried in Danni's arms as she came, and Danni covered her with kisses. Exhausted and spent, their bodies fell limp against each other.

"Well, isn't it a pity I didn't bring my Polaroid?"

The voice came from behind them.

"You fucking closet lesbian, I should have known." It was Anne Yarwood.

Stunned, humiliated, angry, Danni struggled to her feet. "What the hell are you doing here? How dare you walk in here like this?"

"I'm here to talk to Jenny," she said sharply. "Now that you've fucked her ears off, I'm not sure she'll be able to get up off the floor."

Jenny stared dazedly at her.

"Get out," Danni ordered with icy calm.

"So, the town slut's become a switch hitter. What have you two been doing to each other? You should *see* your bodies. You've never come like that with me, Jenny." Anne bit off her words in bitter fury. "Maybe if I roughed you up like Danielle has, you would have."

Danni was aware of Anne taking in her naked body. There was a look of triumph in her eyes — and of accusation.

The years faded and Danni saw her cruel rejection of Anne once more, saw the hurt expression in Anne's eyes as she stood and laughed, smug, safe, on her way to a date with someone she didn't even remember. She could not acknowledge that what she had done then was wrong, utterly wrong. And now? What could this look like but what it was?

"Well, you know how it is, Anne," Danni said, defiantly protecting herself, "it's all the years of practice I've had at one night stands —"

"This is pussy," Anne said crudely. "You can't — I never thought I'd see the day."

"Forget it, Yarwood. As far as I'm concerned, this is just another one night stand."

Jenny stood between the two women looking from one to the other. "What are you *saying*?"

"It's your turn, my sweet," Anne said. "See how you like it."

Jenny looked toward Danni, who wouldn't meet her eyes.

"Danni, listen to your words! A one night stand? Is this how you feel about us? Is it?"

Danni did not answer. She would make this up to Jenny as soon as Anne left.

Jenny ran from the room, up the stairs to the second floor. All she wanted was to get away from Danni, from Anne, away from this unbelievable nightmare. She pulled on a pair of shorts and a shirt and picked up her car keys and wallet. At this point, she didn't know what she was going to do except go after Sara.

"So, Yarwood," Danni said, not acknowledging Jenny's absence, "you finally got your turn."

"To the contrary, Danni." Anne gave her a look of pure malevolence. "It looks like you're the one who finally got *her* turn." Anne left the room and walked quickly to her car.

Danni stood frozen to the spot, paralyzed by her anger. She heard one car back out of the driveway — quickly followed by another.

"Jenny," she cried, "Jenny."

Jenny soon put some distance between herself and Anne. Tears filled her eyes and flowed down her cheeks as she drove toward the quiet, tree-lined lane leading to Ethel Marlowe's house. Who was worse, Anne or Danni?

Anne floored the gas pedal and headed for the highway. She didn't know where she was going; she just knew she had to think and she didn't want to go back to her apartment. She couldn't erase images of Danni and Jenny from her mind. The sounds of their love-making, the passion in their bodies was as vivid to her now as if they were still in front of her, at her feet.

Lust, when newborn, has no equal, and Anne knew she and Jenny had never shared this. What they'd had, she realized, was a comfortable relationship without challenges or choices. Except for the one choice Jenny had made, which was to leave her. Gay life had given her many such endings.

But this was the ultimate irony . . . Danni and Jenny . . . together . . . making passionate love. . . . Anne's hands gripped the steering wheel as again the images rose in her mind. She could feel the anger in her chest and the tears in her eyes. She thought she was going to burst.

Into her fury came one clear thought: That this wasn't the end. There would be a new beginning for her one day — another lover. When, she didn't know — but when it happened, she promised herself that there would be no compromises. She would give all that was desired . . . all that was needed.

Ahead was the Bourne Bridge. Have I come this far, she

asked herself. She looked in the mirror. You look awful, she thought. Then she smiled, ever so slightly. "You'll be all right, Annie," she said. She wiped her tear-stained face, opened the window and took in the fresh morning air.

I might as well drive down to P-town she thought. One way or another, I'll get this out of my system.

XIX

Danni stood in the middle of the destruction she had caused. The chair they'd begun making love on was still turned over on its side. Cups of cold coffee littered the sink. In the bedroom an empty wine bottle, ash trays filled with dead butts, an unmade bed, the smell of sex.

"Yarwood. Anne Yarwood. Why today?" she asked herself. "Why here? We've hardly spoken since college."

That first betrayal was fresh in her mind again. I did the same thing to Jenny, she thought in anguish. I turned on her in the same way. "To save myself," she said aloud. "From what? For what?"

She dressed and went back to the kitchen for a glass and ice. In the living room, she opened a fresh bottle of Scotch. The house seemed so still, so empty. Where had

Jenny gone? Back with Anne? What had she done? What could she do now?

She reached for the phone. "Garth, can you come over? Now?"

"I'll be off duty in half an hour. Is something wrong? Are you hurt?"

"Hurt?" she asked, dully. "No, I just need to see you."

* * * * *

Seeing the back door still open, Garth walked through the kitchen, setting right the overturned chair, and into the living room.

"What's happened to you?" He saw her bruised lip, the glazed look in her eyes. He'd seen her through many bad times, but never had she looked so distraught.

"Did you know that Jenny is a lesbian and Anne Yarwood's been her lover?"

He looked at her carefully. "For some reason," he said, "I'm not surprised. Obviously you were."

"Garth, Jenny's gone."

"To Anne?"

"I don't know. She left this morning. We — I — she and I — Garth, I don't know how to say it."

"Try," he said gently, reaching for her hand.

"I think I'm involved with her." She took a deep breath and admitted, "I know I am. I am. I just don't know what to do. I don't know if she trapped me or tricked me —"

"Danni," Garth said, cautioning her.

"I mean it — I just don't know what happened. I've never been attracted to women, never been to bed with a woman before, never thought I could want a woman."

"Slow down, you're moving too fast for me. Begin at

the beginning."

"It's not easy —"

"Well, you've already given me the big piece of news," he said, thinking of Danni and Jenny making love. The image shocked him. "Now how about telling me how it all happened?"

As she told her story, he remembered the morning after her party. Her concern wasn't for any possible scandal she'd caused, any offense to him or her mother, nor to the rest of their friends, but only for what Jenny thought of the situation, how she could make things right with Jenny. He suddenly saw their domestic summer, their weekend sails in a different light. It would take time to absorb all that she was saying.

"I don't know what to *do*, Garth," she said.

"Calm down, for one thing. Give yourself a chance to think. From what you've said, an awful lot has happened in the last twenty-four hours."

Danni held her glass between her hands and rocked back and forth, back and forth.

She's in bad shape, he thought. Sympathy overcame his shock. He reached for a glass. They both needed a drink.

"Garth, she's *gone*. What should I do?"

He poured Scotch in her glass. "Call Anne," he said.

She looked at him blankly. "Call Anne Yarwood?"

"Yes," he said. It was all he could suggest. He felt helpless in this inconceivable situation.

Danni didn't answer.

"Will you be all right today?" he asked.

She nodded.

"Want me to stop by this evening?"

She shook her head.

"Shall I call you?"

"You don't have to, Garth. I just need time to see my way through this."

"It's going to take time for both of us, don't you think?"

"Oh, yes," she said quietly, "but we're friends, aren't we?"

"Always," he said, meaning it.

"I don't mean to cause the pain I do. You know that, don't you?"

Garth reflected on the years they had known each other. Once again, he realized that he would never be at the center of Danni's life, regardless of how this situation was resolved. "Of course," he said.

As he put down his glass and turned to leave the room, Danni knew she'd hurt him as well.

A dull depression edged the day. Danni stayed close to the phone, hoping Jenny would call. The hours passed slowly. Only once did she consider Garth's suggestion, then she put the notion of calling Anne Yarwood out of her mind.

She couldn't stand being in the house alone any longer. She went out on the *Interlude,* sailing across the bay, remembering other afternoons. She picked out a point on the horizon, sailed toward it, tacked downwind and made her way across the waters.

She felt alive out on the water, confident. I can straighten it out, she told herself. I'll make Jenny understand. If she's back, we'll go out to dinner . . . we'll come home early. Tomorrow we'll have all day together . . . all night together.

As she sailed to her mooring, she felt a euphoric glow that didn't disappear until after she'd secured the boat, returned home and saw that Jenny's car wasn't there.

On Sunday afternoon, Danni couldn't really remember how she'd spent the rest of the weekend. She recalled thinking about going out on a tear, but that she didn't want to be away from the house in case Jenny called or dropped by. She watched TV, she drank, she smoked, she stared out at the sea from the second floor sunroom. She walked through Sara's and Jenny's rooms. She held a sweater of Jenny's and took in its essence.

Much of Saturday night she thought of calling Anne Yarwood. Why couldn't she do it? She looked up her number, dialed the phone, then replaced the receiver. Sunday she made herself a pitcher of martinis. By mid-afternoon she had only one thought in mind: to reach Jenny at Anne's.

She picked up the phone.

"Danni Marlowe here, Anne. May I speak to Jenny?"

"What makes you think she's here?"

"She's not?"

"No, she's not."

"Has she been?"

"No."

"Thanks, Anne."

"For what?"

Her hand tightened on the phone. The martinis hadn't given her as much courage as she wished, but she was determined to try to make peace. "There's no way I can ever make amends, is there?"

Anne didn't answer.

"Not just for this, but before, back at school."

Still no answer.

"I'm sorry for it all," Danni said. "I just want you to know."

"It's been so long I barely remember." The voice was cold.

"I haven't forgotten," Danni said repentantly. "And I wouldn't blame you if you couldn't forgive —"

"Forgive?" Anne asked.

"I don't know what other word to use."

"It's as good as any. That was all years ago, Danni."

"I seem to never stop hurting people. And now look what I've gotten myself into."

Anne didn't reply.

"Look, I'm sorry if I disturbed you."

"That's all right," Anne said curtly. "Goodbye."

Danni held the phone as the dial tone hummed in her ear. She reflected on how she would have felt in Anne's place. Though it was far from adequate, she'd at least made an attempt to come to terms. But what about Jenny? Where was she?

After a sleepless night, Danni decided to get to work early. As she drove the familiar coastal road, she approached her mother's house. She couldn't believe her eyes when she saw Jenny's yellow bug parked in the driveway beside Ethel's Mercedes.

She's here, she thought exultantly, she's here. Of course. Why didn't I think of that?

She geared down to first, pausing for another look at Jenny's car. Then cheered by the knowledge she now had, she drove on into Boston.

XX

Ethel had been upset by Jenny's appearance when she arrived at her home that Saturday. Her hair was uncombed; there was a purple bruise on her cheek. She was distraught, obviously had been crying.

Ethel had seen enough young women in trouble to know that Jenny was in shock. She looked like an abandoned waif, not the beautiful woman Ethel had come to know.

"Jenny, what *happened* to you?" When Jenny didn't answer, Ethel said quietly, "Come with me."

In the kitchen, Ethel filled two glasses to the brim and passed one to Jenny.

"Drink, my dear," Ethel said. "Don't sip."

Jenny raised the glass of wine to her lips and tried to do as she was asked but her hand was shaking and Ethel saw that Jenny was close to tears. Ethel reached across to Jenny and took her hand.

"What happened?" she asked gently. "Tell me."

Grateful for the older woman's warmth and compassion, Jenny poured out her story. She concluded, "Danni turned on me, Ethel. She was like a trapped animal who could only protect herself. She denied me then and there. I didn't know where else to go — I came straight here."

"Does she know you're here?" Ethel asked.

"No. She probably thinks I'm at Beth's."

"Good. If you don't mind, I will not encourage Danni to come here should she call. I think you both need time. Clearly, you need time to heal — not just from these bruises — but from all that's happened. And Danni needs time to see what a terrible mistake she's made."

Ethel expected a call from Danni over the weekend, but perhaps it had not occurred to Danni that Jenny might be here.

By Sunday morning, Jenny was much more in control of herself, much more like her old self, though she seemed sadder than Ethel had ever seen her. Aside from caring for Sara, she spent much of her time alone, looking out one of the large windows at the surf, high this weekend because of the rains and tide.

XXI

When Danni arrived at her office she asked her secretary to cancel all her appointments. Now that she knew where Jenny was, she need only make the right plan for the best way of getting to see her. It wouldn't be easy after what had happened.

I'll be direct, Danni told herself. I'll call her and ask her to have dinner with me tonight. We'll talk, we'll go home, we'll. . . . Her thoughts went no further.

She has to accept my apology. She has to know I'm sorry. She'll see me. I know she will. If she doesn't. . . . Again, her mind went blank.

There's only one way to handle this, Danni told herself. She reached for the phone.

"Mother, I drove by today and saw Jenny's car. Is she

still there? I'd like to speak to her."

"Yes, Danni, she's here. I don't, however, think it would be wise to call her to the phone. She's just begun to seem like herself today."

Danni wasn't sure of how to respond to her mother. Ethel apparently had become Jenny's ally. How much did she know? "I need to talk to her, Mother."

"I'm sure you do. And I'm sure you will. I can tell you, though, that this is not the time. I'll give her your message and you'll hear from her within a matter of days."

"*Days?*"

"Days," Ethel said. "The healing process is slow."

So her mother did know, or at least she knew enough.

"Mother," Danni said slowly, "of all my escapades I would think you'd approve least of all of this one."

Her mother spoke in a quiet voice. "Of all your escapades, Danni, this is the one I would least define as such. We'll talk soon. Goodbye, Danni."

"Goodbye, Mother." Danni sat at her desk to wait for the morning to pass.

Ethel hung up and nodded to Jenny. "You heard what I said, dear."

Jenny walked past her and entered the library. She sat in the large leather wing chair that overlooked the sweep of the bay. She folded her hands and held her knees and began a slow rocking motion, back and forth, back and forth.

In her mind, she turned over the many images she had of Danni: friend and lover, if only for a night. The images blurred. Childishness, vulnerability, destructiveness; where would the pieces finally fall?

Jenny remembered Danni's lovemaking, brutal one moment, tender and passionate the next. What could she expect from her?

The sea was a slate grey sheet, its surface flat as an aged tombstone. Clouds were molten lead hanging low over the horizon. Her thoughts traveled to the sea as if her mind could comprehend its depths.

For a moment, when she and Danni had been together, it was as if their two souls had touched, as if they'd met on ground that would never again be the same. Their souls had bonded, if only for that moment. The ugliness that had followed did not erase the feeling nor make her doubt it, but Jenny knew that what would happen now was out of her hands. Before she could trust Danni again, changes would have to occur within Danni, changes that might not be possible for her to make.

* * * * *

As Danni drove home from work, she knew she wanted to go down to the marina. The sky was overcast and the wind was gentle. If rain was due, it wouldn't fall for several hours. She headed for the boatyard as soon as she'd changed her clothes.

"Think I'll go out for an hour or so," she told Murray as she approached the launch.

"You've pretty much got it all to yourself," he said. "Looks like rain."

"It does," she said. "But I'll get in some sailing before I'm forced to put up my umbrella. Ready?"

"Hop on," he said, casting off.

As she sailed out of the harbor and through the channel, the sea looked thick to her, soupy. Clouds hung heavy in the sky, and thin black cormorants skimming the water looked like prehistoric birds.

This wasn't an afternoon for pleasure sailors. Around Grape Island she spotted several small fishing boats. A lobster boat motored by to check traps. She waved to a young man in a plaid shirt and yellow rubber overalls. She sailed close enough to one of the fishing boats to find out they were in the midst of a school of blues.

A fog had started to mist the air; none of the buildings that formed the usual skyline were visible. She decided to circle Grape, then head back, but first she locked the tiller, let out the sheet line a bit, and opened a bottle of brandy. It was smooth and warmed her body. She was glad she'd brought it along.

Sitting under the sky, feeling a kinship with the fishermen around her, she realized a sense of calm for the first time in days. I'll see it through, she thought. I'll wait, however long it takes. As long as she's at Mother's, she's not going anywhere. Mother will take good care of her, I know.

Danni watched lobster traps being hauled out of the water. The lobsters were swiftly released and put in carriers, then the baited traps were lowered back into the sea. A sea breeze ruffled her hair, light wisps brushing her cheek, and she remembered Jenny's tenderness. Memories of their passion were vivid in her mind.

I want her again, Danni thought. She'll have me; I know she will. We're not like Yarwood and women like her. This is just between us. No one else needs to know. Anne won't talk. She won't want to admit she's lost her lover.

I'll bet lots of women have these arrangements. Garth is understanding, he'll keep it to himself. Mother's broadminded . . . apparently more so than I realized. And we've got enough skeletons in our family closet that the bones won't rattle too much if the story does get out. But it *won't*. Who would ever suspect Jenny and me? No one will ever know.

I'll take her and Sara abroad for the holidays. She can see men now and then if she wants. I know I'm not about to give them up — maybe for now but not forever. In fact, we *should* keep seeing men. That'll be our cover.

Who am I kidding? Who needs a cover? Have I ever worried about my reputation before? But face it, Danielle, this is different. We'll just play the game and no one will be the wiser.

Danni tightened her sails. A swift wind took her quickly into the harbor and to her mooring. She let down the sails, tidied up, and while she waited for Murray to come out for her, she had another nip of brandy. She went home in high spirits, fully expecting the phone to ring sometime that evening. It didn't.

XXII

With only two weeks before the beginning of her own classes, Jenny was determined to find as much of an answer as possible for her dilemma.

Beth Drew told her of an apartment in Boston available for a year's sublet. She and Beth drove into the city to see it, and even though Sara would have to transfer schools, Jenny decided it would provide a solution to part of her problem.

"I'm not *going*," Sara said when Jenny broke the news. "I want to go back to Danni's. I miss her, I miss Duvall. I'm not going. You can't make me." Sara's eyes filled with tears and she curled her little fingers into tight, angry fists.

Jenny reached for Sara's hand but she pulled away.

"You don't like Danni anymore," she said. "I *love*

Danni." And Sara ran from the room.

There was no way to even begin to explain this to Sara. Perhaps time would help this situation as well; Sara would simply have to accept the new circumstances of their lives.

* * * * *

As Danni pulled into the driveway, she sensed that something was different. Usually, Duvall's bark greeted her. Carefully, she walked around the outside of the house to see if anything was amiss.

She smiled. In the back yard, beside the swing set, Duvall was stretched out on the grass. And next to him, her arm wrapped around his neck, was Sara, fast asleep. When Duvall saw Danni, he made an attempt to sit up, but Danni's pat on the head assured him to stay put. Danni sat down next to Sara and gently picked her up, hugging her close. As Danni rocked her back and forth, Sara sleepily opened her eyes.

"Hi, sleepyhead. It's nice to see you."

"Can I stay with you?" Sara asked. "Can I live here with you and Duvall?"

"Why, sure, honey, you do live here, don't you remember?"

Sara sat up and hugged Danni. Her arms wound so tightly around Danni's neck that Danni wondered at her strength.

"I love you so much, Danni. I ran away. I walked here all by myself and nobody knows where I am. I'm not going away. Mommy can't make me, can she?"

Danni held her close and tried to soothe her, at the same time hearing the loud pounding of her own heart. I'll lose both of them, she thought, both of them at once. I can't let it happen.

"Sara, just don't you worry. I'll straighten everything out. Trust me?"

Sara nodded, hugging her close. Danni took her hand and led her into the house.

As Danni picked up the phone, a distraught Jenny burst into the room. "Sara," Jenny said, "to the car. Now. Right now. And sit there and wait for me. *Don't* wander off."

Sara looked at Danni.

"Do as your mother says," Danni said. "And remember what I said."

Sara did as she was told.

Danni was mesmerized by the sight of Jenny standing before her. There were dark circles under Jenny's eyes; she seemed to have lost weight, but she looked extraordinary to Danni, precious beyond belief. Danni smiled and walked toward her; there was no smile in return.

"Sara told me you're leaving Baysville. You can't go until we talk."

"What do you have to say?" Jenny asked sharply.

"Just listen," Danni said. "I know what you must think of me after the other morning. I don't know what happened to me. But I don't want you to leave. I've been thinking; there must be plenty of women like us, women who share a life with each other, who live together —"

"There are," Jenny answered, her tone softening. Was Danni actually speaking these words, she asked herself. This was all she had hoped for . . .

"Nobody could ever guess about us. No one would ever know. It'd be our business, right? We could still see men when we wanted to — hell, you must have the urge every now and then."

"What are you talking about?" Jenny stared at Danni in disbelief.

"About *us*. Look at the life we could have — we could

travel, enroll Sara in the best private schools, you can take your time finishing school, go on for a master's if you like. I've got the agency. What more could we want?"

"You don't know what you're saying, do you?" Jenny asked in a cool, hurt voice. "You haven't learned a thing about this. Or a thing about yourself, when it comes down to it."

"I know what I like," Danni said.

"A one night stand?"

"I didn't mean that."

"And you think what you're describing is ideal?"

"Why not? What's the problem?"

"I don't have any problems, Danni. You're the one who can't face up to what this is all about. I know who I am. Can you say that about yourself?"

"What do you mean?"

"I'm a lesbian, Danni. What are you?"

"I'm not — that. You're not either. You like men. Sara's proof of it. I've seen lesbians all my life and I know that neither one of us should be pigeonholed. If we can have the best of both worlds, why not?"

"Danni, I don't want to play games. I don't have to play games. What I want is an honest, monogamous relationship with the woman I love. I'll spend the rest of my life looking for it if I have to. What you want is a farce."

Danni moved toward her. "Jenny, think about it — about everything. You remember how it felt, don't you? You remember how good it was for both of us. That's what *I* want again. And so do you."

Danni put her trembling hands on Jenny's shoulders. Her blood was pounding in her ears. Her hands ran down to Jenny's waist; she pulled Jenny toward her and rubbed her back like a lifeguard trying to put life back into a rescued swimmer. Kissing her neck, her mouth, her eyes, Danni pressed her body, hard and hot, against Jenny's; her tongue prodded Jenny's lips. She reached for the zipper of Jenny's slacks. Danni's breath was rapid, heavy. She brushed her lips against Jenny's neck. The sensation was of kissing cold marble.

"If you're going to take me," Jenny said, her words quick, angry barbs, "do it quick — here — up against the wall. I don't want to leave Sara in the car much longer."

Danni backed off and looked at the stranger before her.

"Why don't you just go out and get yourself a few more one night stands?" Jenny flung at her. "Maybe you can interest someone else in your domestic arrangement."

Jenny ran out to the car. She felt sick. This was no victory. She was leaving the woman she loved. Danni had too far to travel, too far to go. It had taken her years to bring herself to this point. Danni had not even begun to find out what she was about. They were too far apart.

As she opened the car door and looked at Sara, she almost burst into tears. But as calmly as she could, she said, "Everything will be all right soon. I promise you."

Sara examined her face then stared straight ahead and didn't say a word.

XXIII

The early morning tide had turned as sunlight scattered lacy patterns across the water. Aside from a stray dog wandering behind her, Jenny had the beach to herself.

She spotted a piece of driftwood, tossed it and watched the dog run after it. She buttoned her sweater, put her hands in her jeans pockets and kept walking. The air coming in off the water was cool. Fall, it's almost here, she thought. She shivered thinking of the season that she always found a little sad. A lone sailboat cruised the waters.

The morning passed as Jenny walked the sands. She thought: I've got to decide soon. If I walk away, I'll lose her. If I take her on her terms, it's a charade.

It's not fair to Sara. It's not fair to me. Sara's lost too much already; our separation, the divorce, the move up here. She's got a right to be angry, Jenny thought, recalling Sara's sullen moods this week, her silence.

I've got to turn this situation around and get us moving. Somewhere. As she looked out over the water, she had a vision of Danni: sun-burned, wind-blown, tired from a long day on the boat, but contented and happy. If nothing else, she had that memory.

It just isn't fair. She could feel the anger she'd held inside; she wasn't sure if she was angrier at herself for loving Danni or at Danni for what she had suggested. She couldn't have expected me to accept her on those terms, she thought. How could she have? Yet when the fantasy of Danni became the reality of the woman she knew, Jenny realized that there was nothing else she could have offered at the moment. So then, why run away?

There had to be some place in Baysville for Sara and her, some kind of work she could do. Ethel was willing to help; why not let her? And somehow, in the next few days, she would see Danni. They would talk.

* * * * *

Danni motioned to the bartender to bring her another martini.

What a mess, she thought. So what was so bad about what I offered her? What'd she expect? Towels monogrammed with our initials? Easy enough for her to be so casual about all this — she didn't grow up in Baysville. She doesn't run a business in Boston. She'd be a little more cautious if this were her home town. But then again *would* she? Danni was struck by the thought.

Even though Jenny had concealed her relationship with Anne, even though she had felt deceived by Jenny's tactics, she believed that Jenny had planned to end things with Anne before their own relationship had gone any further than it had. She wished she could talk to Jenny now about how Jenny had come to make all her choices. How many years had it taken? And had the miles of her journey been difficult?

The bartender set down the fresh drink. "Sure you want this?" he asked.

"I wouldn't have ordered it if I didn't, Jeff," she said. "But thanks for the message. Pass me the check and I'll head on out of here."

At home, she wandered through her empty house. She stood in front of Jenny's loom and ran her hands over an intricate design. She picked up Sara's teddy bear from the floor and put it on the shelf.

Danni sat on the second floor sunporch. The word lesbian came into her mind. She allowed herself to think about it, running the syllables repeatedly over her tongue.

Les-bi-an; lover of women. Lover.

I love a woman, she thought.

I love Jenny.

I love.

Feeling the power of those words for the first time in her life, she cried. Tears flowed freely down her cheeks and in the darkness she felt not sorrow, but peace.

Through the night, she was conscious of hours passing as she watched the moon cross the starlit sky, casting its reflection on a calm and velvet sea.

I can feel her so close, Danni thought, it's as if she's here. Wherever she is, whatever she's doing, she must *know* how much she means to me.

She awakened early the next morning, still sitting on the sunporch, and saw the first trace of daylight, a thin line of light in the sky, then the red rim of the sun, and finally the clouds, blue sky, a pink morning.

Thoughts flowed into her as if directly from the night before. I'm in love with Jenny and I know she loves me. I'll tell her that I want to be her lover, that I love her. That we have as much a right to a life together as any two people and I don't care what label I wear.

Maybe I've botched things so far, but there's no way I'm going to let that woman walk out of my life.

* * * * *

Later that morning, needing to buy coffee at the market, she closed the back door, leaving Duvall inside. As she passed the garage, she noticed the three speed boy's bike Jenny had bought at a flea market when she and Sara had first moved in. Impulsively, light-hearted with the knowledge that she would see Jenny today, Danni hopped on, pedaling exuberantly down the driveway and onto the road.

It was a leisurely ride to the village; the morning air was fresh. As she neared the village awash in morning sunlight, it was as if she were seeing its quaint charm for the first time. She pedaled down Main Street and into the parking lot of Murphy's Market. She hopped off the bike and leaned it against the side of the small brick building. She thought about what else they might need besides coffee. What else *I* might need, she amended. It's all going to take time; I'd better face up to that first of all.

Danni picked up a pound of coffee, a carton of cigarettes, and walked to the checkout line. She stopped in her tracks as she saw Jenny, only a few feet away, standing in line. She walked toward her, brushing past the shoppers who separated them.

"Hi," Danni said.

Jenny turned, and as Danni smiled, she felt as if they

were standing on an empty street, as if she and Danni were the only ones there.

Their eyes met and held. Danni wondered: Whatever made me afraid of admitting that I love her?

"I love you," she said, softly.

"What?" Jenny asked, wanting to believe the words she had just heard, wanting to hear them again.

"I love you," Danni repeated, gazing at her.

"You do?"

"I do. I'm *in* love with you. What do you think about that?"

"I think it's exactly what I want to hear." She grinned and squeezed Danni's arm. "I'm in love with you, too."

"You're not leaving town?"

"I was going to call you and tell you . . . I'll find an apartment nearby for Sara and me, and a job, I hope. Then I want us to begin seeing each other."

An elderly gentleman with two items in his arms moved ahead of them in the checkout line. "Excuse me, ladies," he said. "The missus is out waiting in the car."

"See each other?" Danni asked, not even looking at him. "What are you talking about? I want you to come home with me right now."

"Just like that?"

"Just like that. Everything you said the other day was true. I've got a long way to go. I've got so much to learn. But I want you with me, at home. You and Sara."

"You girls all set?" the woman behind the cash register asked. "You're holding up the line, you know."

"I know I'm ready," Danni said, smiling. "How about you, Jenny?"

"Oh, yes," Jenny said, "I'm ready."

As they collected their change and picked up their bags, Danni asked, "Are you coming back?"

"That depends," Jenny said teasingly.

"On what?" Impulsively, Danni kissed her cheek.

Jenny laughed. "Can you cook?"

They walked toward the door. Danni said, "Jenny, you know I can't." Then she looked at her and smiled. "But how'd you like to teach me?"

Outside the market, Danni took Jenny's hand. She led her to the blue bicycle as if she'd been riding it all her life.

"Hop on."

Jenny saw that she wasn't kidding. She sat on the crossbar.

Slowly, Danni pedaled out of the parking lot and onto Main Street. She was having a hard time balancing the two of them, but knew if she took her time she'd make it. Danni nuzzled Jenny's hair as Jenny leaned her body comfortably into hers.

"Want to stop at your mother's and pick up Sara?"

"I don't think so," Danni said. "Why don't we just go on over to our place? After all, everyone's entitled to a honeymoon."

As they stopped for the traffic light at the corner of Spring and Main Streets, Jenny turned and kissed Danni on the lips.

The Long Trail by Penny Hayes. A western novel. 248 pp.
ISBN 0-930044-76-2 $8.95

Horizon of the Heart by Shelley Smith. A novel. 192 pp.
ISBN 0-930044-75-4 $7.95

An Emergence of Green by Katherine V. Forrest. A novel.
288 pp. ISBN 0-930044-69-X $8.95

The Lesbian Periodical Index edited by Clare Potter. 432 pp.
ISBN 0-930044-74-6 $24.95

Desert of the Heart by Jane Rule. A novel. 224 pp.
ISBN 0-930044-73-8 $7.95

Spring Forward/Fall Back by Sheila Ortiz Taylor. A novel.
288 pp. ISBN 0-930044-70-3 $7.95

For Keeps by Elisabeth C. Nonas. A novel. 144 pp.
ISBN 0-930044-71-1 $7.95

Torchlight to Valhalla by Gail Wilhelm. A novel. 128 pp.
ISBN 0-930044-68-1 $7.95

Lesbian Nuns: Breaking Silence edited by Rosemary Curb and
Nancy Manahan. Autobiographies. 432 pp.
ISBN 0-930044-62-2 $9.95
ISBN 0-930044-63-0 $16.95

The Swashbuckler by Lee Lynch. A novel. 288 pp.
ISBN 0-930044-66-5 $7.95

Misfortune's Friend by Sarah Aldridge. A novel. 320 pp.
ISBN 0-930044-67-3 $7.95

A Studio of One's Own by Ann Stokes. Edited by Dolores
Klaich. Autobiography. 128 pp. ISBN 0-930044-64-9 $7.95

Sex Variant Women in Literature by Jeannette Howard Foster.
Literary history. 448 pp. ISBN 0-930044-65-7 $8.95

A Hot-Eyed Moderate by Jane Rule. Essays. 252 pp.
ISBN 0-930044-57-6 $7.95
ISBN 0-930044-59-2 $13.95

Inland Passage and Other Stories by Jane Rule. 288 pp.
ISBN 0-930044-56-8 $7.95
ISBN 0-930044-58-4 $13.95

We Too Are Drifting by Gale Wilhelm. A novel. 128 pp.
ISBN 0-930044-61-4 $6.95

Amateur City by Katherine V. Forrest. A mystery novel. 224 pp.
ISBN 0-930044-55-X $7.95

The Sophie Horowitz Story by Sarah Schulman. A novel. 176 pp.
ISBN 0-930044-54-1 $7.95

The Young in One Another's Arms by Jane Rule. A novel.
224 pp. ISBN 0-930044-53-3 $7.95

The Burnton Widows by Vicki P. McConnell. A mystery novel.
272 pp. ISBN 0-930044-52-5 $7.95

Old Dyke Tales by Lee Lynch. Short stories. 224 pp.
ISBN 0-930044-51-7 $7.95

Daughters of a Coral Dawn by Katherine V. Forrest. Science
fiction. 240 pp. ISBN 0-930044-50-9 $7.95

The Price of Salt by Claire Morgan. A novel. 288 pp.
ISBN 0-930044-49-5 $7.95

Against the Season by Jane Rule. A novel. 224 pp.
ISBN 0-930044-48-7 $7.95

Lovers in the Present Afternoon by Kathleen Fleming. A novel.
288 pp. ISBN 0-930044-46-0 $8.50

Toothpick House by Lee Lynch. A novel. 264 pp.
ISBN 0-930044-45-2 $7.95

Madame Aurora by Sarah Aldridge. A novel. 256 pp.
ISBN 0-930044-44-4 $7.95

Curious Wine by Katherine V. Forrest. A novel. 176 pp.
ISBN 0-930044-43-6 $7.50

Black Lesbian in White America by Anita Cornwell. Short stories,
essays, autobiography. 144 pp. ISBN 0-930044-41-X $7.50

Contract with the World by Jane Rule. A novel. 340 pp.
ISBN 0-930044-28-2 $7.95

Yantras of Womanlove by Tee A. Corinne. Photographs.
64 pp. ISBN 0-930044-30-4 $6.95

Mrs. Porter's Letter by Vicki P. McConnell. A mystery novel.
224 pp. ISBN 0-930044-29-0 $6.95

To the Cleveland Station by Carol Anne Douglas. A novel.
192 pp. ISBN 0-930044-27-4 $6.95

The Nesting Place by Sarah Aldridge. A novel. 224 pp.
ISBN 0-930044-26-6 $6.95

This Is Not for You by Jane Rule. A novel. 284 pp.
ISBN 0-930044-25-8 $7.95

Faultline by Sheila Ortiz Taylor. A novel. 140 pp.
ISBN 0-930044-24-X $6.95

The Lesbian in Literature by Barbara Grier. 3d ed. Foreword by
Maida Tilchen. A comprehensive bibliography. 240 pp.
ISBN 0-930044-23-1 $7.95

Anna's Country by Elizabeth Lang. A novel. 208 pp.
ISBN 0-930044-19-3 $6.95

Prism by Valerie Taylor. A novel. 158 pp.
ISBN 0-930044-18-5 $6.95

Black Lesbians: An Annotated Bibliography compiled by
J. R. Roberts. Foreword by Barbara Smith. 112 pp.
ISBN 0-930044-21-5 $5.95

The Marquise and the Novice by Victoria Ramstetter. A novel.
108 pp. ISBN 0-930044-16-9 $4.95

Labiaflowers by Tee A. Corinne. 40 pp.
ISBN 0-930044-20-7 $3.95

Outlander by Jane Rule. Short stories, essays. 207 pp.
ISBN 0-930044-17-7 $6.95

Sapphistry: The Book of Lesbian Sexuality by Pat Califia. 2nd
edition, revised. 195 pp. ISBN 0-930044-47-9 $7.95

All True Lovers by Sarah Aldridge. A novel. 292 pp.
ISBN 0-930044-10-X $6.95

A Woman Appeared to Me by Renee Vivien. Translated by
Jeannette H. Foster. A novel. xxxi, 65 pp.
ISBN 0-930044-06-1 $5.00

Cytherea's Breath by Sarah Aldridge. A novel. 240 pp.
ISBN 0-930044-02-9 $6.95

Tottie by Sarah Aldridge. A novel. 181 pp.
ISBN 0-930044-01-0 $6.95

The Latecomer by Sarah Aldridge. A novel. 107 pp.
ISBN 0-930044-00-2 $5.00

VOLUTE BOOKS

Journey to Fulfillment	by Valerie Taylor	$3.95
A World without Men	by Valerie Taylor	$3.95
Return to Lesbos	by Valerie Taylor	$3.95
Odd Girl Out	by Ann Bannon	$3.95

I Am a Woman	by Ann Bannon	$3.95
Women in the Shadows	by Ann Bannon	$3.95
Journey to a Woman	by Ann Bannon	$3.95
Beebo Brinker	by Ann Bannon	$3.95

These are just a few of the many Naiad Press titles. Please request a complete catalog! We encourage and welcome direct mail orders from individuals who have limited access to bookstores carrying our publications.